"You!" the thug yelled, and pointed the gun at Callie.

"Callie!" She heard the panic in Seth's voice. Then a force like being tackled by a linebacker slammed into her, and she landed in the seat of the booth with Seth shielding her body. A bullet whizzed over the top of the booth and struck the far wall.

She waited for the second shot, but all she heard was the banging of the front door. In the next moment she could hear Seth speaking into his lapel mic.

"Suspect armed and on his way out the front door." He ran toward the door. He'd just reached out to open it when gunfire from outside split the air. He jerked the door open and ducked as a bullet shattered the door frame above his head.

Guilt welled up in her and sucked the breath from her body. What had happened outside? Had her presence tonight compromised Seth's stakeout, and was he lying on the sidewalk injured, or even worse, dead?

She had to find out.

Books by Sandra Robbins

Love Inspired Suspense

SANDRA ROBBINS,

former teacher and principal in the Tennessee public schools, is an award-winning multipublished author of Christian fiction who lives in the small college town where she grew up. Without the help of her wonderful husband, four children and five grandchildren who've supported her dreams for many years, it would be impossible to write. As a child, Sandra accepted Jesus as her Savior and has depended on Him to guide her throughout her life. Her writing ministry grew out of the need for hope she saw in the lives of those around her.

It is her prayer that God will use her words to plant seeds of hope in the lives of her readers so they may come to know the peace she draws from her life verse, *Isaiah* 40:31—"But those who hope in the Lord will renew their strength. They will soar on wings like eagles, they will run and not grow weary, they will walk and not be faint."

Trail of Secrets

Sandra Robbins

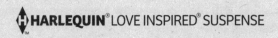

HARLEQUIN® LOVE INSPIRED® SUSPENSE

Recycling programs
for this product may
not exist in your area.

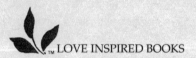™ LOVE INSPIRED BOOKS

ISBN-13: 978-0-373-67607-1

TRAIL OF SECRETS

Copyright © 2014 by Sandra Robbins

www.Harlequin.com

Printed in U.S.A.

Are not two sparrows sold for a farthing? and one of them shall not fall on the ground without your Father. But the very hairs of your head are all numbered. Fear ye not therefore, ye are of more value than many sparrows.

—*Matthew* 10:29–31

ONE

From the first moment Callie Lattimer spotted her uncle, U.S. Federal Judge Dan Lattimer, waiting for her outside the security area at Memphis International Airport, she knew something was wrong. He barely kissed her cheek before he hurried her toward baggage claim and then to his car. As they sped through the night along Interstate 55 toward his home in midtown Memphis, the light posts on the side of the road appeared to fly by the car windows.

His hands gripped the steering wheel so tightly that his knuckles turned white, and the muscle in his jaw flexed. When he glanced in the rearview mirror again as he'd been doing ever since they left the airport, Callie could hold her tongue no longer. "Uncle Dan, what's the matter?"

His body tensed further, and he cast a surprised look in her direction. "What do you mean?"

"I can tell you're upset. Has something happened I need to know about?"

He shook his head. "No. I'm just a little preoccupied over a case."

Callie reached over and squeezed his arm. "You're not supposed to be worrying about a case, not with your retirement a week away."

"I know, but old habits are hard to break." He glanced in the rearview mirror again.

"You're going to have to break those old habits. I'm here to spend the summer with you, and I want us to enjoy our time together, especially our trip to Hawaii."

His forehead wrinkled. "We will, darling. I just have to get some things worked out before we can go. In the meantime, I've booked you a room at the Peabody. I think it would be better for you to stay there for a few days until I get this case cleared up."

Callie sat up straight and swiveled in her seat to face him. "What? I don't want to stay at the Peabody. I want to stay at home."

"You will. Like I said, just give me a few days, then we'll get started on our summer plans."

"But Uncle Dan…"

"Oh, no!" her uncle exclaimed, his wide-eyed stare locked on the rearview mirror.

Behind them Callie heard the roar of a car

engine as it pulled into the passing lane. She turned her head to look over her shoulder, but her uncle's big hand gripped the back of her neck and pushed her face down to her lap as their car surged forward in a new burst of speed. Callie tried to wriggle free of the tight grip, but it was no use.

The crack of gunfire split the air, and the glass on the driver's-side window shattered. Uncle Dan's hand loosened then fell off her neck completely, and the car swerved toward the road's shoulder. Callie glanced up to see her uncle slumped over the steering wheel, his hand now hanging limply beside him. Before she could reach out to him, the car hit the highway guard rail, which folded like an accordion. Her air bag released and pushed her back into her seat as the car flipped on its side and plunged down a small embankment.

The vehicle's jarring stop knocked the breath from Callie's chest, and she closed her eyes as dizziness engulfed her. After a moment she swallowed, opened her eyes and took a deep breath.

Somehow the car had righted itself before it came to a stop, and she struggled to sit up in her seat. She turned her head to the side and gasped at the sight of her unconscious uncle behind the driver's-side air bag. Blood poured down the side of his face. She pushed her air bag out of the way and fumbled to release the seat belt, but it wouldn't open. "Uncle Dan!"

She touched his neck, found his weak pulse and groaned. He needed immediate medical attention. Her purse with her cell phone inside had been next to her feet before the crash, but it could be anywhere in the car now. She swept the floor with her hand but couldn't find it. She glanced back at her uncle, but he still hadn't moved. Blood from his head wound covered the now-deflating driver's-side air bag and dripped to the floor.

She grasped the handle, pulled it back and shoved her shoulder against the door, but it wouldn't budge. "Help!" she screamed. "Somebody, please help us!"

The sound of raised voices reached her ears, and relief flowed through her. Just as quickly it turned to fear. What if the shooter was coming to finish them off? With them trapped in the car, they were perfect targets. Panicked, she shoved on the door again.

A man's face appeared at the shattered driver's-side window, and he peered inside. "Are you all right?"

In the darkness she couldn't make out his face, but the man's voice had a soothing quality. "Yes, but my uncle is hurt."

"I've called 911," he said. "Help will be here any minute to get you out of there." The man reached through the window and touched her uncle's chest. "He's breathing. Now you just take it easy until we get some help."

Callie leaned back in her seat and breathed a sigh of relief. "Thank you for helping us."

"I'm glad I saw your car run off the road. I thought that car passing you got too close. Then I heard a loud noise like a gunshot. Whoever was driving that car meant to hurt you."

Callie nodded. "Yes, it looked that way to me, too."

"Now don't you worry. I'll stay right here with you until help arrives. It shouldn't be too long."

Convinced they were safe for the moment from the person who'd tried to kill them, she closed her eyes. This wasn't the homecoming she'd expected. She'd been looking forward to Uncle Dan's retirement celebration for weeks. He'd worked so hard for years, first as a Memphis police officer while enrolled in law classes at night, then as a Memphis attorney and finally as a federal judge. He had spent the better part of his life bringing criminals to justice. If anyone deserved a peaceful retirement, he did.

Callie had opted out of teaching summer classes at the University of Virginia where she was a professor in the School of Business so she could spend the entire summer with him. They were set to celebrate his retirement the way he'd planned for years—in a Maui beach house they'd rented for six weeks.

She clenched her fists and rubbed her temples. It wasn't fair. He was the best man she'd ever known, and he'd dedicated his life to raising her when she was left with no one. In just a few days he'd be able to leave the stress of his job behind and enjoy life for a change. He wasn't supposed to wind up wounded and bleeding for reasons she didn't understand while his attacker got away.

The sound of sirens pierced the air. Callie opened her eyes and looked toward the road. "They're here," the man beside the car said.

He'd hardly finished speaking before she saw the flashlight beams of the first responders bobbing in the darkness as their rescuers came down the embankment. The man who'd been talking to her moved out of the way as one of the rescuers stopped beside the car. He glanced at her uncle, then at her. "Don't you worry, ma'am, we'll have you out of there in no time and on your way to the hospital."

Thirty minutes later an EMT carried her up the embankment to the ambulance with its flashing lights. She eased over to the gurney where her uncle lay and grasped his hand. He hadn't responded to anyone since he was pulled from the wreck.

She glanced up at the EMT who had just finished checking his pulse. Even though she feared the answer, she had to ask the question burning in her thoughts. "Is he going to be all right?"

The EMT adjusted the oxygen cannula in her uncle's nose and frowned. "It's still too early to say, ma'am. The doctor can tell you more when we get both of you to the hospital. Even though you appear to be unhurt you need to be checked out, too. You can ride in the back with your uncle."

Before they could load the gurney into the ambulance, her uncle stirred, and his eyelids fluttered open. She clutched his hand tighter and leaned closer. "Uncle Dan, it's Callie. Can you hear me?"

"Callie." The hoarse whisper seemed to exhaust him.

"Yes, I'm here. We were in a car wreck. We're going to the hospital. Everything is going to be all right."

He frowned and licked his lips. "Call Seth."

Callie clutched her uncle's hand tighter and shook her head. "Uncle Dan, don't talk. Just lie still."

His eyes grew wide, and he struggled to push up. "No!" he wheezed. "Need Seth. Something to tell him about the case."

She glanced up at the EMT who placed his hands on her uncle's shoulders and eased him back down to the gurney. "All right, Uncle Dan. I'll call Seth."

"Tell him it's important," he mumbled before he closed his eyes again.

New tears poured down Callie's cheeks as she watched her uncle being loaded into the ambulance. One of the EMTs grasped her arm to help her up, but she paused when a car skidded to a stop next to the police car blocking the highway, and a man jumped from inside.

She wouldn't have to call Seth after all—he was already here.

She braced herself for her first encounter with Seth Dawtry since the night when she'd turned down his marriage proposal. For years her uncle had said that she and the young policeman he'd mentored would make a perfect couple. He'd tried matchmaking every time she came back to Memphis to visit. It had almost worked two years ago.

Seth only hesitated a moment when he saw her standing at the back of the ambulance before he raced toward her.

"Is he alive?" His voice shook with each word.

She nodded. "Yes, but he's seriously injured. How did you know he'd been hurt?"

"One of the first responders is a friend of mine. He called as soon as he saw who it was. I got here as fast as I could." He glanced at the EMT inside the ambulance. "Is he conscious?"

The man shook his head. "He was for a moment but not now."

She took a deep breath and turned toward Seth. "He asked me to call you. If he regains consciousness, I'll tell him you arrived."

Seth's eyes narrowed, then his stare settled on her and turned cold. Even after two years she could see he still harbored anger toward her. He gave a curt nod. "Thanks."

She tried to smile but her lips trembled. "We need to go."

Seth backed away. "I'll follow the ambulance to the hospital and see you there."

Callie wanted to tell him there was no need for him to go to the hospital, but she knew he would never listen to her. His relationship with Dan had been forged years ago when Seth was a recruit at the Memphis Police Academy where Dan was an instructor. They'd bonded right away, and in Dan, Seth had finally found a father to replace his own who had abandoned their family. Dan also regarded Seth as the son he'd never had.

She nodded and climbed in beside Dan's gurney. Before they could close the door, one of the men who'd pulled her from the car ran up to the ambulance. "I found your purse in the backseat," he said. "I thought you might need it."

Callie took her purse and smiled. "Thank you. I appreciate everything that all of you have done for us tonight."

He touched the front of his helmet in a small salute. "It's part of the job, ma'am. I'll be praying for you and your uncle."

The ambulance door closed before she had a chance to respond, to tell him how those words from a man she'd met only minutes ago had comforted her. She glanced down at her uncle lying so still on the gurney and wrapped her fingers around his big hand. One of the EMTs grabbed the rear doors to close them, and Callie glanced over her shoulder. Seth had already disappeared from view.

Still holding his hand, she dropped down in the seat across from her uncle. When she'd arrived at the Memphis airport an hour ago, she hadn't expected this turn of events. The memory of a roaring car and a gunshot blast flashed in her mind, and she closed her eyes and groaned.

Then there was her brief meeting with Seth. She'd been resigned to bumping into him at Dan's retirement party, but had hoped she could avoid any extended conversation. So much for that plan. Now he would be at the hospital, and she would have to keep him informed of her uncle's condition.

He'd tried to hide it, but even after two years she could feel his smoldering anger toward her. Perhaps he never would forgive her for how she'd hurt him, but she had hoped by this time he had moved on. She'd put the events of two years ago behind her, but it didn't look like he had.

Her uncle's body jerked suddenly and gasping sounds came from his throat. The EMT grabbed her uncle's hand out of her grasp and pressed his finger to the pulse. Frightened, Callie scooted away to give the attendant more room to work in the crowded ambulance.

"What's happening?" she cried.

Without answering her, he turned and yelled to the driver. "We have a problem back here. Move it!"

The ambulance surged forward, and Callie could only watch in horror as her uncle struggled to breathe. The vehicle careened into the hospital parking lot and came to a screeching halt at the emergency room bay.

Before she could ask another question, the back doors opened, and the ambulance driver reached up to help the EMT whisk the gurney out of the ambulance. A nurse helped Callie to the ground, seated her in a wheelchair and hurried toward the entrance.

The EMTs had the gurney inside before Callie and the nurse got to the doors. When they entered the waiting area, Callie grasped the arms of the wheelchair and choked back a sob at what she saw. Two nurses and the EMTs ran down the hallway beside her uncle's gurney. Before she could call out to them, they made a sharp turn and disappeared into a room on their right.

The nurse turned the wheelchair toward the exam rooms on the other side of the area. Callie sat up straight. "Where are you taking me?"

"To an exam room," the nurse said.

"But I want to be with my uncle."

The nurse shook her head. "I'm sorry, but you can't do that."

"Why not?"

The question was no more than out of her mouth when she saw the answer in the nurse's eyes. She couldn't be with him because he was dying.

Seth Dawtry's heart sank as he pulled his car into the emergency room's parking lot. An ambulance, its rear doors still open, sat backed up in the bay for unloading patients. He knew enough to know that if they'd abandoned the ambulance to rush the patient inside, things weren't looking good.

He pulled the car to a stop and sat there a moment, grasping the steering wheel, trying to work up the will to go inside. As badly as he wanted to know his friend's condition, he couldn't bring himself to move. Not when it meant facing Callie.

He'd known Dan was picking Callie up at the airport tonight, but he hadn't expected to see her so soon. In fact, he'd planned to stay as far away from her as he could while she was in town. But his anger toward Callie was no reason to abandon Dan right now.

He would be polite to Callie because Dan would want that. But as soon as Dan was out of danger, he'd go back to keeping his distance. With a sigh, Seth said another quick prayer for Dan before he jumped from the car and sprinted toward the entrance.

The automatic doors parted as he barreled toward them, and he ran into the waiting room that was packed with people waiting to be seen by a doctor. It seemed that no matter what time of day or night his job brought him here on an emergency, the area was always crowded with patients. Tonight, though, he wasn't here on police business. This visit was personal.

He hurried over to the receptionist's desk, but

the young woman who sat there didn't look up from her computer as he came to a stop. "How can I help you?" she asked.

He pulled out his badge and held it toward her. "I'm Detective Seth Dawtry with MPD. I'm here about Judge Dan Lattimer and his niece who were just brought in. They were in a car wreck on I-55 coming from the airport. Can you give me any information?"

The girl glanced at the badge and then at him. "They arrived a few minutes ago. If you'll have a seat, I'll go check on them for you."

"Thank you." Seth backed away from the desk and looked around for an empty chair. They all appeared to be occupied, so he stuck his hands in his pockets and walked to the edge of the room.

Within minutes the young woman was back, and he hurried to her desk. "I talked with the doctor. He's examining Miss Lattimer now. When he's finished, you can go back and talk with her."

Seth nodded his thanks and walked back to the spot where he'd been standing. For the next fifteen minutes he forced himself to stay still and not give in to the urge to pace up and down the room. After what seemed like an eternity, the young woman motioned for him to follow her. She opened the door and pointed down the hallway.

"Miss Lattimer is in the third treatment room on the right."

Seth smiled at her. "Thanks."

He took a deep breath and started down the hall. The closer he came to where Callie waited, the slower his steps grew. He'd often wondered if he would ever see Callie again, but he would never have thought they'd meet because Dan was near death. He needed to keep reminding himself that his anger toward Callie didn't matter right now. His reason for being here was Dan's welfare, and he could stand to be around her if it meant he could help his friend in any way.

A curtain blocked his view into the glass cubicle, and he paused a moment. "Callie," he said, "it's Seth. May I come in?"

"Yes." Her soft voice was barely audible.

He pulled the curtain back and stepped into the room. She sat on an exam table with her legs hanging over the side. It might have been two years since he'd last seen her, but he remembered how beautiful she'd looked that night— right up to the time she told him she wouldn't marry him and had run from the room. Tonight she looked very different. Her long, dark hair was pulled back in a ponytail, her eyes were red and puffy from crying, and her mascara had left dark smudges on her cheeks.

The expression on her face left little doubt to the seriousness of Dan's condition. "H-how is he doing?"

A big tear rolled down her cheek. "It's not good, Seth. He almost quit breathing before we got to the hospital. The doctor came by a few minutes ago and said they'd inserted a breathing tube. They're taking him to surgery in a few minutes. They don't know if he'll make it or not."

Seth almost doubled over from the crushing pain that exploded in his chest. He took a step closer to her. "No!" he said. "He's supposed to retire, not die."

Her shoulders began to shake, and she dissolved in tears. "I know. We had such big plans for our summer. Now all I want is for him to live so I can tell him how much I love him."

Seth wished he could say something to make her feel better. But even if he knew what to say, she probably wouldn't appreciate it, coming from him. He jammed his hands in his pockets and cleared his throat. "And how are you doing?"

She wiped at her eyes and sighed. "I'm fine. The doctors checked me out and said there were no broken bones or internal injuries. Uncle Dan took the worst of it all." Her eyes filled with tears again. "He pushed my head into my lap and held it there to protect me."

"That sounds like Dan," he said. He took a step closer. "We're going to get this guy, Callie. The FBI will join the Memphis Police Department on this case, and I'm sure the U.S. Marshals will be here shortly to offer protection for Dan. You don't have anything to worry about except taking care of yourself and Dan."

"Thank you, Seth."

The curtain parted, and a doctor stepped into the room. He glanced from Seth to Callie before he spoke. "Miss Lattimer, we're ready to take your uncle to surgery. Would you like to see him before he leaves?"

"Yes, I would."

Seth watched her hop down from the table, and then the two of them stepped into the hall where two nurses stood beside Dan's gurney. Seth didn't move as they stopped beside his friend.

Callie leaned close to him and whispered in his ear. "I love you, Uncle Dan. I'll be waiting for you when you come from surgery." She kissed him on the cheek, jammed her fist into her mouth to stifle her sobs and stepped away from the gurney.

Seth bent over and touched Dan's shoulder.

"I'm here, Dan. I promise you I'll get whoever did this to you."

For one brief moment, Dan's eyes blinked open, and he stared up at Seth before he darted a glance at Callie and then back to Seth. A look of desperation lined his face. Once more he cut his eyes to Callie and back to him, and Seth knew Dan was trying to send him a message.

Seth's eyes filled with tears, and he nodded. "Don't worry about Callie, Dan. I'll take care of her."

Dan's eyes drifted closed, and the nurses pushed the gurney down the hall. When it disappeared through the doors that led to the elevators for the surgery floor, Callie began to sob.

Seth searched his mind for something to offer her comfort. Finally, he decided she needed to get out of this area and to a place that might offer some peace. He reached out and touched her arm. She jerked her head up and stared wide-eyed at him.

"It's not going to be easy waiting," he said. "Why don't we go down to the hospital chapel? Maybe being in that quiet room will help calm you down some."

She frowned. "I'm not very religious."

He nodded. "I know. That was something else we never saw eye to eye on, but like I tried to tell you then, it's not about being religious. It's about finding some peace in life. How about it? You might find it helps to be in a more soothing place for a while."

She brushed her hands across her eyes and glanced around the stark emergency room. "Okay. I guess it can't hurt."

A nurse stepped out of an adjoining exam room at that moment, and Seth told her where the doctor could find them before he led Callie out of the emergency room and into the hospital proper.

When they arrived at the chapel, he opened the door and held it for her to enter. As he stepped into the room behind her, he closed his eyes for a moment and let himself relax into the peace that being in this place evoked in his soul. A table with a cross and an open Bible on it sat at the front of the room, and he led her to seats directly in front of the display.

They sat without speaking for a while until she finally broke the silence. "This is much better than the E.R. It's quieter and more peaceful. Thank you for bringing me here."

"I've been in this room a lot in the past few years."

She turned her head, a questioning expression on her face. "Oh? How so?"

He sighed and rubbed the back of his neck. "This is where we bring families when they're waiting to hear if their loved ones will survive after a violent crime. It's a peaceful place, and we hope it can afford the families some measure of comfort."

Tears pooled in her eyes. "Is that why you brought me here?"

"Partly. But I wanted to ask you about the shooting, too. I don't want to cause you any more stress than you're already under, but I thought it might be easier to talk about it here than in the hustle and bustle of the emergency room."

She nodded. "I think it is, but there's something I need to know, too."

"What's that?"

She inhaled a deep breath. "From the moment Uncle Dan picked me up I could tell something was wrong. He kept looking in the rearview mirror, and it seemed he almost suspected something was about to happen. When the EMTs were loading him in the ambulance, he opened his eyes long enough to tell me to call you. He needed to tell you something."

Seth frowned. "Did he say what it was?"

She shook her head. "No. But he had to be restrained on the gurney because he was so determined there was something important he had to tell you about the case, he said. Has he been helping you with a case you're working on?"

Seth's stomach curled with fear at Callie's words. After a moment he shook his head. "No, I've been helping *him* with a case for the past year or so."

"I don't understand. What kind of case would he need help with? He's not a policeman anymore. He's a judge, and judges don't investigate cases."

Seth stood up and paced to the far wall before he turned and walked back to stand in front of her. Dan had mentioned several times that Callie knew nothing about the case he'd worked on for years because he knew she would be upset he was investigating a murder. It had been something he didn't share with many of the people in his life. Seth happened to be the exception to the rule. But it was time Callie knew, especially if that case was the reason Dan was in surgery fighting for his life.

He dropped back in his chair and nodded. "I guess it's time you learned about the burden Dan has carried for years. He knew you would try to persuade him to give up if he told you about it, so he never did."

Callie clasped her hands in her lap and swallowed hard. "What kind of case is it?"

He spread his hands in a helpless gesture and shook his head. "I can only tell you what Dan has told me. This case dates back to when he was on the police force."

She sat up straighter, her eyes wide. "On the force? But that was years ago."

Seth nodded. "Twenty-five years, in fact. One morning he was called to the banks of the Mississippi River just south of downtown where a woman's body had washed up. She looked to be in her early thirties, and she'd been shot. There was no identification on the body, but Dan felt sure that as pretty and as well dressed as she was, someone would report her missing."

"Did they?" Callie asked.

Seth shook his head. "When he didn't hear anything, he went by the medical examiner's office and learned she didn't fit the description of anyone who'd been reported as missing in Memphis. That made him wonder if she was from somewhere else. He asked about her personal effects, and they gave him an envelope that only contained a locket she was wearing. Inside was the picture of a little boy who looked to be about five or six. Then he asked to see her body. That's when something strange happened to him."

"What?"

"He said he stood there and looked down at her and there was something about her face that reminded him of your mother."

"My mother?" Callie's question was barely more than a whisper.

"Yes. He said your mother had died a few weeks before, and you had just come to live with him. You'd cried the night before for your mother, and he wondered if the little boy in the picture in the locket was crying for his mother. So he made a pledge to the dead woman that he wouldn't rest until he'd found her family and returned her body to them. When no one ever came forward to claim the body, Dan bought a burial plot and a tombstone and had the woman buried at his own expense. For the past twenty-five years, every time he read or heard about a missing woman, he'd check it out to see if it was his victim, but it never has been."

"He had her buried and a tombstone placed at her grave?"

"Yes."

"What name did he put on the tombstone?"

"Since he didn't know her name, he decided to give her one. He thought she deserved more than Jane Doe. She needed a special name, so he put the name Hope on her tombstone."

"Hope?"

"Yes. He said it was a name that fit his feelings toward her—hope that he could return her to her family. Through the years, every time he grew discouraged and ready to give up, he'd visit her grave. Seeing that name on her tomb-stone would remind him that somewhere there had to be somebody hanging on to the hope that their wife or mother or daughter would be re-turned to them. And he'd promise her again that he wouldn't give up. He would find her killer, and he'd return her to her family."

Callie nodded. "That sounds like Uncle Dan. He's got such a good heart. All he wanted to do was help someone, and now it looks like his good intentions may have put him in danger." She was silent for a moment. "I can't believe Uncle Dan never told me about this case."

"It became a very personal cause with Dan to return her to her family. He knows you have issues over your father's death and his involve-ment in law enforcement. He wanted to distance you from the things in his life that haunted him so you could be happy in the life you'd chosen. He tried to do everything he could to make that happen."

"I know." She unclasped her hands and rose to her feet. "And yet all that time he was trying to make my life better, he was obsessed with re-turning this woman to her family. I wish I had known so I could have made it easier for him."

Seth stood and faced her. "Don't blame your-self, Callie. This is the way he wanted it. But now that things have turned dangerous, you need to know what's at stake. I only hope if he has found out something, he'll be able to tell me what it was. I'd like to bring closure to the case that Dan has never been able to walk away from—and I'd like to see whoever did this to Dan brought to justice."

She nodded. "I hope you can. What happens if he dies? Will anyone else take the case?"

"I work in the Cold Case Unit now with two partners, and we'll keep it on our radar. After all, that's our job, working cold cases."

She bit down on her lip and thought for a moment before she spoke again. "You're right. That's what you do. But it's not what he does anymore."

Seth regarded her with a questioning gaze and frowned. "What do you mean?"

She balled her hands into fists and clenched them at her side. "Uncle Dan hasn't been a policeman in over twenty years. He shouldn't have put himself in danger like this."

Tears flowed down her face, and Seth rose to his feet. "What are you saying, Callie?"

"I'm saying if he lives I'm going to insist on some changes. First of all, I'm sure there will be a long recuperation time. I think it would be best if I took him back to Virginia with me. I can see that he gets all the help he needs, and

I'll be there to take care of him. Maybe there he can put this case behind him."

Seth shook his head. "As long as there's breath in Dan's body, I don't think he'll be able to put this case out of his mind."

"You don't understand!" she cried out. "I lost my father when he tried to stop a guy on drugs from robbing a convenience store. Now it's possible this murder that happened twenty-five years ago is the reason my uncle is fighting for his life. I can't lose him, too, like I lost…"

She stopped, and a look of panic crossed her face. Seth nodded. "Were you going to add me to that list, too? Were you going to say like you lost me because you couldn't bring yourself to marry a policeman?"

Callie jumped to her feet and clenched her fists at her sides. "This is no time for us to discuss our past, Seth. My uncle's survival is the most important thing now."

After a moment, he nodded. "You're right, Callie. Whatever we once had died two years ago, but I don't think Dan will give up on this case as easily as you did on us."

She glared at him before she dropped back in her chair, propped her elbows on her knees and buried her face in her hands. Seth stared at her and then glanced up at the clock. Eight-thirty. He sighed. It was going to be a long night.

Four hours later, Seth stopped pacing the floor and turned toward the door when it opened. Callie glanced over her shoulder, then slowly rose to her feet. Seth moved to stand next to her.

The doctor stepped into the room and stopped when he saw them. Tired lines etched his craggy face, and his wrinkled, green scrubs hung on his slender frame. He pulled the surgery cap from his head and sighed.

Beside him, Seth heard a mewling groan in Callie's throat, and he grasped her arm to steady her as the doctor walked toward them.

TWO

It's bad news. I know it is.

The thought wouldn't quit running through Callie's mind as the doctor came closer. She wished she could put her fingers in her ears and not hear what he was about to tell her, but that wasn't practical. She felt Seth grab her arm, but she couldn't turn her head to look at him.

"Miss Lattimer?"

"Yes, I'm Callie Lattimer."

The doctor stopped in front of her. The green surgery mask dangled from his hand. "I'm Dr. Singer. I've just finished operating on your uncle."

Callie hadn't thought it possible, but her heart rate increased. "H-how is he?"

Dr. Singer rubbed his hand across the top of his head. "He made it through surgery, but he's not out of the woods yet. He's fortunate that the EMTs arrived so quickly, especially since he almost quit breathing on us. But on the way here they were able to stem some of the blood flow, which is very important in wounds of this nature. Another favorable factor in his case is that the tract of the bullet doesn't seem to be extensive. There is good brainstem function, which gives me hope that if he survives, his rehabilitation may not be too extensive."

Seth's hand tightened on her arm and then released. He exhaled a deep breath, and she knew he was as relieved to hear the news as she. "Oh, Dr. Singer, this is good news."

He held up his hand in warning. "Don't get me wrong. There are still a lot of things that can go wrong. We're moving him to the Critical Care Unit to monitor him. There is some swelling of the brain, and I've removed a portion of the skull to relieve the pressure. We can take care of that later if all goes well. The next few weeks are critical."

Callie nodded. "I understand. When can I see him?"

"Now, if you want to. He's settled in the unit, and the nurses there will let you in for a few minutes. Then you should go home and get some rest. You've been through a lot tonight, and you've got some tough days ahead."

"I understand, Doctor. And thank you for what you've done."

He smiled. "I'm glad I could be of service. I'll see you in the morning."

Callie turned back to Seth as the doctor left the chapel. "Would you like to go with me to see Uncle Dan?"

"I would, and then I'll drive you to Dan's house."

"You don't have to do that. I can get a cab."

He frowned. "I don't mind."

"No, really, Seth. You don't have to do it."

He gritted his teeth and raked his hand through his hair. "I said it's okay, Callie. After all, I promised Dan I'd take care of you, and I'm not going back on my word to him."

His words snaked out toward her, and she reeled as if he'd slapped her. Of course, he wasn't doing it for her. It was because he'd promised her uncle. She nodded. "I understand. Thank you for offering to take me home." They turned to walk to the door, but Callie stopped after taking a few steps. "Oh, I forgot. My luggage is still in Uncle Dan's car. Is it possible to get it tonight?"

"I'm sure we can. Captain Wilson is on duty. I'll call him right now and see where they towed the car, then I'll take you by there to get your bags before I drive you home. Go ahead and check on Dan, and I'll meet you in the E.R. waiting room."

"Thanks, Seth. I appreciate it."

They stopped at the elevator, and Seth pushed the button. When the doors opened, he stepped back to let her enter. "I know Dan will be unconscious, but tell him I'll see him in the morning."

"I will."

As Callie approached the Critical Care Unit, she noticed a room on the left side of the corridor. People, who she assumed to be family members of patients, lay in lounge chairs in the room. A young woman in a nurse's uniform rose from behind a desk as she entered.

"May I help you?"

Callie nodded. "Dr. Singer told me my uncle has been brought to Critical Care and I could see him. His name is Dan Lattimer."

The young woman smiled. "Yes, he's here. I'll be glad to take you in."

She came around the desk and led Callie through the double doors at the end of the hall. Callie had never been in a unit like this before, and she didn't know what to expect. She swallowed and stepped into the long room with a hallway that ran in front of glassed-in cubicles. A nurse's station faced the small rooms. Monitoring machines hummed in the otherwise silent ICU, and shivers ran up Callie's arm.

A man in a dark suit sat in a chair outside one

of the small cubicles, and he rose when she approached. "Miss Lattimer?"

"Yes."

"I'm Deputy U.S. Marshal Chris White. I'm here to guard your uncle. Dr. Singer told me you'd be coming up."

Callie glanced past him into the small room behind the marshal. She saw someone in the bed, but with all the bandages she couldn't tell if it was her uncle or not. She swallowed past her nausea and stared at the still form. "Is that my uncle?"

"Yes," the marshal said. "You can go in."

Callie hesitated a moment before she stepped inside and inched toward the bed. He was covered with a white sheet, but his arm lay motionless at his side. She placed her purse in a chair at the foot of his bed, eased up beside him and covered his hand with hers.

One of the machines monitoring his vital signs beeped, and she glanced at it. She had no idea what all the numbers displayed stood for, but she did know as long as they were showing up it meant her uncle was alive. Her gaze drifted over the pale face almost covered with bandages and she brushed at the tears that flooded her eyes.

"I'm here, Uncle Dan, and so is Seth," she whispered. "The doctor says you came through the surgery fine. If I know you, you'll be up and about before we know it. I wanted to see you before I went home to get some rest, but I'll be back in the morning. You have a good night. I love you."

She wanted to stay with him, to watch over him as he had done so many times when she was a child and sick, but she knew it wouldn't be allowed in this unit. She had to trust his well-being to people who'd been trained to care for critical patients. She fought back another rush of tears as she leaned over and kissed him on the cheek before she stepped outside and stopped next to the marshal. Before she could speak, an alarm sounded, and two nurses who'd been at their station when she entered earlier suddenly ran to a cubicle several doors down from her uncle's.

Her eyes grew wide. "What's happening?"

The marshal nodded in the direction of the commotion. "It looks like one of the other patients is having some problems."

"Then I'd better leave. Thank you for watching over my uncle, Marshal White. Maybe I'll see you again."

"We'll have a marshal on him until the shooter is caught. Don't worry about him. Go on home and get some sleep."

She smiled, turned and walked out of the unit.

As she headed toward the elevator, she thought of Seth waiting downstairs and was glad he said he'd drive her to collect her luggage from Uncle Dan's car. Getting in his house shouldn't be a problem because she still carried a key to the front door on her key ring. She punched the button for the elevator and froze in place.

Her purse. It was still in the chair at the end of Uncle Dan's bed. She must really be tired if she hadn't realized she'd left without it.

With a groan, she retraced her steps to the Critical Care Unit. She glanced in the waiting room as she passed by and came to a sudden stop. Marshal White stood beside the vending machine, drinking a soft drink. He glanced her way and smiled. "What are you doing back?"

She frowned. "I forgot my purse. Why are you out here?"

He swallowed a sip of his drink. "One of the nurses needed to check Judge Lattimer's vital signs and said it would be okay for me to get something to drink while he was busy in the room."

Callie frowned. "I didn't see a male nurse while I was in there."

Marshal White shrugged. "I think he'd just come down to help them since that other patient was having problems."

Callie nodded. "Do you think it would be okay for me to step in and get my purse?"

"I think so. Go ahead."

She walked to the entrance into the unit and only hesitated a moment before pulling the door open. Once inside, she looked toward the room where the nurses had been working earlier. Since there was no one at the desk, she assumed they were still busy with the patient, and she eased toward her uncle's room.

The curtains had been pulled around the cubicle, blocking sight into the room. Her first thought was that it was probably standard procedure when they were working with a patient, but she frowned when she noticed that the curtains hadn't been pulled in the room where the nurses still worked. She tiptoed to her uncle's space, pulled back the curtain and slipped into the room.

A nurse was bent over his bed and didn't seem to hear when she entered. She spotted her purse and was about to reach for it when she froze in place. Fear shot through her body like a bolt of lightning. The nurse wasn't administering any kind of aid. Instead, he was holding a pillow over her uncle's face.

With a loud scream, she sprang on the man's back and grabbed him around the neck. His body jerked in surprise, and he twisted to free himself. "What…?" he yelled as he reached up and grasped her hands.

Callie screamed again and clawed at the surgical mask covering the man's face. It slipped from his mouth, and Callie glimpsed a jagged scar down the right side of his face. The mask slipped farther, and she caught sight of a star tattoo on his neck.

The attacker hunched his shoulders and heaved with enough force to knock Callie from his back. She sailed backward and hit the wall with a loud thud. The man whirled, pulled a gun from his waistband and aimed it at her. Before he could pull the trigger, Marshal White appeared in the doorway, his gun drawn.

"Hold it right there!" he yelled.

The attacker whirled and pulled the trigger. The sound echoed off the walls, and Marshal White slumped to the floor. The shooter lunged for the door, jumped over the marshal's body and sprinted down the hallway. Callie rushed to the door and caught sight of him as he ran through the exit at the far end of the hallway. Realizing she wouldn't be able to catch him, she turned back in time to see the two nurses who'd been cowered against the wall outside the other patient's room straighten up.

One of them pushed to her feet and glanced

at her coworker. "I'll check the marshal and the judge. You call security and get us some help."

The other one ran to the nurses' station and picked up the phone while the one who'd spoken knelt next to Marshal White. She looked up at Callie. "What happened?"

"There was a man in scrubs trying to suffocate my uncle. If I hadn't come back for my purse, he'd be dead now."

The nurse nodded and called out to the other one. "The marshal needs to get to surgery right away. I'll check Judge Lattimer."

Callie stood in the cubicle, unsure what to do as nurses and security guards poured into the unit. She glanced from her uncle to the marshal on the floor before she picked up her purse and sat down in the chair where it had lain.

Around her it seemed as if some kind of ordered chaos erupted. Nurses bent over her uncle, checking his vitals. A gurney appeared beside the marshal, and within minutes he was whisked away to surgery. A security guard stood behind the nurses' station, barking orders into a mike attached to the lapel of his shirt.

She rubbed her hands over her eyes and shuddered. When was this nightmare going to end? One of the responders glanced up from checking her uncle and jerked her head toward the door. "You need to wait outside until we finish here."

Callie took a deep breath, straightened her shoulders and shook her head. "I'm not moving from here until there's someone else from the U.S. Marshal's office at that door. If it wasn't for me, my uncle would be dead right now."

The nurse started to respond, but then she just smiled. "I guess you're right. I wouldn't want to leave, either. Is there anyone we need to call for you?"

"Detective Seth Dawtry is waiting for me in the E.R. I'd appreciate it if someone would ask him to come up here."

"I'll take care of it," the nurse said.

Callie watched her walk to the nurses' station before returning her attention to her uncle. The picture of a man with a pillow over her uncle's face flashed in her mind, and she began to tremble. For the second time since her plane had touched down in Memphis, someone had tried to kill her uncle. After what Seth had told her about Uncle Dan's cold case, she knew it had to be the reason behind the attempts.

She rose, walked over to the bed and grasped her uncle's hand. "Uncle Dan, what have you gotten yourself into?"

Seth ended the call to Captain Wilson and slipped his cell phone back in his pocket. It hadn't taken long to find out that Dan's SUV had been transported to an all-night tow service in midtown. Captain Wilson said Callie's bags had been taken out of the car and were waiting in the business's office to be picked up. Now if she would just come on, he might be able to get her settled at her uncle's and get himself home in time for a little sleep before going back to work in the morning.

He glanced at his watch and frowned. He hadn't expected Callie to be gone so long, but he could understand her reluctance to leave her uncle. Perhaps he should have gone back upstairs with her. Dan might have taken a turn for the worse.

He yawned and had just dropped down in a chair when a voice blared over the intercom system. "Security stat! Security stat!"

Seth bolted to his feet and let his gaze sweep the room. He knew what that alert meant. Security was shutting down the hospital because of a threat somewhere. Could it have something to do with Dan?

At that moment, a hospital security guard ran into the waiting room and stopped at the receptionist's desk. "Have you seen a man in scrubs run through here in the past few minutes?" he demanded. Before she could answer, Seth pulled out his badge and ran over to the man.

"What's happened?"

His eyes scanned the badge before he responded. "Someone tried to kill a patient in the Critical Care Unit."

A groan rumbled in Seth's throat. He ran from the room and raced to the stairs. He didn't have time to wait for an elevator. When he burst into the fourth-floor hallway, his knees grew weak at the activity outside the unit. Bleary-eyed people huddled in small groups in the waiting room. He'd been here enough on the job to know they were family members who spent long nights as close to injured loved ones as they could get. Nurses scurried around, and two security officers guarded the entrance to the Critical Care Unit.

He ran toward the guards with his badge held high. "Detective Seth Dawtry, MPD. Has something happened to Judge Lattimer?"

One of the men held up his hand, and Seth skidded to a stop next to him. "There's been an attempt on his life. His niece interrupted it and called for help, but when the marshal who was guarding him intervened, he was shot and has been taken to surgery."

Seth's heart constricted. He glanced into the waiting room in hopes of seeing Callie, but she wasn't there. "Where's Judge Lattimer's niece?"

The security guard inclined his head toward

the unit. "She's in with her uncle. Do you want to see her?"

"Yes."

The man opened the door, and Seth rushed in. Callie, her purse clutched in a death grip, sat in a chair at the foot of her uncle's bed. She turned a tear-stained face toward him as he entered. "What happened?"

He listened in disbelief as Callie related the events of the past few minutes. When she finished, she shook her head and groaned. "They almost succeeded this time, Seth. Uncle Dan was just seconds away from death."

Her body trembled, and he reached for her hand. "Then we have to be thankful you left your purse. Have you heard anything from the marshals yet?"

As if in answer to his question, the door to the unit swung open, and Rob Grant rushed into the room. He stopped next to Seth. "I was on my way here when I received a call that the judge had been attacked and our marshal had been shot."

Seth nodded. "They've taken your marshal to surgery, but Dan is okay." He glanced at Callie. "This is Rob Grant. He's the U.S. Marshal for our district. Rob, this is Callie Lattimer, Dan's niece."

Rob reached for Callie's hand. "I can't tell

you how sorry I am about this, Miss Lattimer. Hospital security tells me you saved your uncle's life. You never should have been put in that position. Can you tell me more about what occurred?"

She quickly related what had happened. "I'm sorry about Marshal White, though. I hope he's going to be all right."

Rob exhaled a long breath. "I hope so, too. He's new to our office, and he made an error in judgment. I'm so sorry it almost ended in tragedy. That won't happen again. I'm going to stay until another marshal comes to take over, and you can be assured we won't let your uncle out of our sight again."

"Thank you. I appreciate your help."

Rob glanced at Seth. "I'm sure Miss Lattimer is tired. There's nothing else she can do here tonight. Why don't you take her on home?"

"I think I'll do that," Seth said. "Are you ready to go, Callie?"

A tired smile pulled at her lips. "I am."

She glanced at her uncle once more before she turned and walked out of the Critical Care Unit. They stopped at the elevator and pushed the button, but when the door opened, Captain Wilson of the Memphis Police Department and two officers stepped off.

Callie's eyes lit up when she saw her uncle's

best friend and former partner. She threw her arms around his neck, and he pulled her close. "Anthony," Callie said, "it's so good to see you."

He pulled back and stared down into her face. "I've been trying to get over here ever since I was notified about Dan being shot, but I'm on duty all night. It's been one of the busiest nights I've had in a long time. But when the call about Dan's attack in the ICU came in, I broke all speed records getting here. What happened?"

He shook his head in dismay as Callie told what had happened when she walked into her uncle's room. "I didn't think before I jumped on the man's back. He was twice as big as me, but I knew I had to stop him," she said.

Captain Wilson's gaze raked her body. "Are you okay? Did he injure you in any way?"

"No, I'm fine."

"Then what can you tell me about the man? Was there anything that would help you identify him if you saw him again?"

She nodded. "When I wrapped my arms around his neck, the medical face mask he was wearing slipped to the side. He had a jagged scar that ran down the right side of his face from about the bottom of his ear to his chin. And he had a star tattooed on his neck."

"Was there anything else? Was he short? Tall? Skinny? What was his coloring?"

Callie thought for a moment before she responded. "Dark hair and tan skin—maybe Latino, but I can't be sure. He was about Seth's height, and he was very muscular. He had broad shoulders, and I felt his muscles flex when he threw me off. He reminded me of the guys you see constantly working out in a gym."

Captain Wilson nodded. "Good. That ought to help us." He smiled at her. "You've done well tonight, Callie. You survived two shootings and you fought someone who seemed intent on killing your uncle. It's good to see that it's not only the men in the Lattimer family who can hold their own with the bad guys. You can, too."

She laughed and shook her head. "I don't think so, Anthony. I just want to teach school. I'll leave chasing crooks to men like you and Seth."

He smiled. "I think you've had enough excitement for a while. You go on home now. I need to talk with Rob Grant and make sure nothing like this happens again." He turned to Seth. "Can you see that Callie gets home?"

"I will, sir."

Without another word, Captain Wilson strode down the hallway and through the doors of the Critical Care Unit. The elevator doors opened again, and Seth and Callie stepped inside. Neither of them said anything until they had exited the hospital and stood in the parking lot outside the E.R. Seth pointed across the rows of cars to where his sat underneath a lamppost. "That's my car over there."

He led her to his car and unlocked the door for her to crawl in before he walked around to the driver's side and slipped behind the steering wheel. He glanced over at her as he started the car, but she had her head resting against the back of her seat and her eyes closed. He thought she must have been asleep before they drove from the parking lot.

Thirty minutes later he stopped in the driveway of Dan's house and placed his hand on her shoulder. "Callie," he said as he gently shook her, "we're at your uncle's house."

She sat up, rubbed her eyes and looked around. "I'm sorry. I must have fallen asleep." She reached for the door handle but frowned and hesitated. "I thought we were going to get my bags."

He laughed and opened his door. "Already done, ma'am. You were sleeping so soundly I didn't wake you for the pickup. I have your bags in the trunk. I'll take them in and check the house before I leave."

He started to get out of the car, but she reached out and touched his arm. "Seth, I really do appreciate all you've done for me tonight."

Seth smiled. "No need to thank me. Dan is special to me." He didn't mention the way that Dan had filled the void in his life after his father walked out on them when he was a boy. Back when he'd dated Callie, he'd told her the whole story, about how he'd always envied his friends who had fathers who came to their ball games and had time to take them fishing or work on cars in the backyard. He'd never had anything like that until Dan became the father he needed. Tears threatened to fill his eyes, and he turned his head to stare out the car window so she wouldn't see.

"I know," she said. "He's often told me you're the son he never had. After I went to college and on to graduate school, I didn't come home very much. I should have. I know he was lonely at times and I'm glad he had you." Her voice broke on the last words.

"Don't blame yourself for anything," Seth replied. "He's proud of you and what you've made of your life. He tells everybody about his smart niece who's got her Ph.D. and is a big-time professor at the University of Virginia."

She chuckled. "I don't know about the big-time part, but I do love my job."

"Just as Dan and I do ours, Callie. Try to remember that."

She stared at him for a minute before she took

a deep breath and opened her car door. "I get your point, Seth, but nothing's changed since we last saw each other."

"I know," he said. "I've moved on, and I hope you have, too."

She regarded him for a moment before she spoke. "I have. Now I'd appreciate it if you'd check out the house before you go. I don't want another encounter with Scarface tonight."

"You've got that right," he said as he stepped out of the car. "I'll do a walk-through and then be on my way, but I'll come back tomorrow and take you to the hospital." He glanced at the clock on the dash. "Since it's nearly three o'clock in the morning, tomorrow will be here before we know it."

She nodded and headed toward the house. "I don't think I'll have any trouble falling asleep."

She'd already opened the front door by the time he arrived on the steps with her bags. He put them down in the entry and proceeded to search the house before he let her enter.

As he walked through the rooms, Callie's heart sank to the pit of her stomach. The house exuded a hollow feeling as if her uncle's absence had sucked out all the life it usually possessed. Seth must have felt it, too, because she knew it had become the home away from home he'd come to love.

He stopped just inside the den, and his gaze raked the room. Then she saw his lips move and knew he was offering a prayer for his friend's life. Callie turned away and shook her head. That was something else she and Seth had never shared, and she doubted they ever would.

Ten minutes later she stood at the front door and watched Seth get in his car. Then she locked the door and walked back into the living room. The lamp by the window she'd turned on when she'd first entered the house still lit the room.

She turned the light off and stood there in the dark room for a few minutes, staring out to the quiet cul-de-sac where she'd first learned to ride her bicycle. Sweet memories of her uncle holding her upright until she learned to balance drifted into her head, and a tear slipped down her cheek.

She was about to turn away when the lights of an approaching car caught her attention. It moved so slowly she wasn't sure whether she imagined it or not when it seemed to come to a stop in front of her house.

A small circle of red lit the interior for a brief second. A lit cigarette. Callie's skin prickled at the feeling that someone inside that car had stopped to study her uncle's house. After a minute, the car moved slowly to the end of the street and made a circle in the cul-de-sac before driving past her uncle's house once more.

This time she studied the outline of the vehicle more carefully. Her knees trembled, and she grabbed the table to steady herself. Was this the car she'd caught a fleeting glimpse of before Uncle Dan shoved her head into her lap?

THREE

Callie rose in bed and pounded her pillow again in an effort to get more comfortable. Her statement that she wouldn't have any trouble falling asleep had come before a strange car had stopped in front of her uncle's house. Even though she had watched it drive away, every time she closed her eyes, she either relived the gunshot blasting into the car, the scene of a man with a pillow over her uncle's face or a dark car with its engine idling in front of the house.

She glanced at the cell phone lying on the bedside table and sighed. Four a.m. It would probably be sunup in an hour or so, and she hadn't slept a wink. Groaning, she sat up on the side of the bed and rubbed her tired eyes. She wouldn't be able to keep her eyes open at the hospital when she went back later today, but she couldn't help it. Her raw nerves refused to let her relax, and she climbed out of bed.

She put on her robe, slipped her cell phone in her pocket and went downstairs. Maybe a glass of warm milk would help her fall asleep. After heating some milk, she carried the cup into the den and sipped at it as she stared out the window into the backyard.

The tree she'd climbed as a child seemed to wave its branches at her as she stared into the darkness. She smiled, remembering the times she had called for her uncle, who was usually busy in his office next to the den, to come watch her climb one branch higher. He had always answered her summons. She still had trouble believing he'd been just as devoted to an unsolved case.

She paused in remembering and turned her head to stare at the door leading from the den into the office. That room was where he kept all his important papers. Could there be something in his desk that would help her understand his obsession with the case she'd learned about tonight?

Easing into the room, she switched on the light, placed her cup of milk on the desk and sat down in the chair behind it. She spread her hands out over the smooth wood on the desktop and closed her eyes for a moment. She could almost feel the presence of the man she thought of as her father.

After a moment, she opened the right-side top drawer, but there was nothing inside except a collection of pens and pencils along with a stapler and an assortment of rubber bands. The drawer below held odds and ends, too. When she opened the bottom drawer, which looked to be the deepest, there were only a few papers lying inside.

She was about to close it when something strange caught her eye. The drawer appeared deeper than the two above it, and yet it had little room inside to hold items. She leaned closer and stared at the interior before pulling the papers out and tapping on the bottom of the drawer. A hollow-sounding noise told her the drawer had a false bottom.

She grabbed a letter opener from the desktop and slipped it between the edge of the bottom and the side of the drawer. The bottom of the drawer sprang open to reveal a large three-ring notebook inside.

Her heart pounded as she pulled out the notebook and laid it on the desk. With shaking fingers, she opened it and gasped at the picture of a woman, her eyes closed in death, on the first page. Tears filled Callie's eyes as she read the caption written in her uncle's familiar handwriting underneath the picture.

Hope
You will never be forgotten.

Callie swallowed her tears and turned the page. Entries that followed described the discovery of the body on the banks of the Mississippi River, the medical examiner's report and facts about the investigation. It seemed every detail that had been known about "Hope" at the time of her death was listed on the pages. What pricked Callie's heart was the fact that nothing about her identity had been added in the years since.

She turned to the next section and read through what appeared to be hundreds of reports on missing persons near Hope's determined age who had disappeared from various parts of the country about the same time as she had. Each entry contained notes on the victim, her uncle's contact with the families and his conclusion that this wasn't a match to the woman he was looking for.

She frowned as she leafed through the thick stack of reports. He'd spent endless hours through the years tracking down dozens of leads, but nothing had yielded the identity of the one he'd buried in Memphis twenty-five years ago.

Callie had never stopped to think about the number of people who disappeared in this country every year. Her uncle had known, though, and he had cared. She turned back to the picture of Hope and stared at it again. Who was she? Where had she come from? And how did she end up dead in the Mississippi River? Those thoughts must have run through her uncle's head every day.

She noticed a piece of paper that looked different from the others sticking from the back of the notebook, and she turned to it. It was a flyer advertising a homeless shelter near downtown. The name Dorothy Tipton, written in her uncle's handwriting, was paper-clipped to the flyer. What was that about?

She turned another page and frowned at the names listed with phone numbers beside them. She read through the names, but she'd never heard of any of them. One near the bottom had a check mark next to it, and she stared at it. Melvin Harris. Who could he be? She made a mental note to ask Seth if he knew the man.

Closing the notebook, she sat there a moment thinking about what she'd found out tonight. Even though the news of her uncle's secret case had surprised her, she had a different feeling toward it now. Hope had been a real person to him, a woman whose dreams and desires had been cut short by a killer. He wanted justice for her, and he'd tried to give it to her. Now he might not get to do that. Before, she'd felt only worry for her uncle, but now she understood a little better how much this case had meant to him. She was glad to think that Seth could continue her uncle's work. She'd turn the notebook over to him when he came by in the morning.

She took the last drink of her milk and was about to return the notebook to its drawer when the sound of shattering glass from the direction of the kitchen ripped through the house.

She bolted to her feet and glanced wildly around to see if anyone came charging into the den. Another crash split the air, and a new fear engulfed her. She grabbed the edge of the desk to steady herself. Hissing and popping sounds mixed with the odor of an accelerant could only mean one thing.

Someone had thrown a fire bomb into the house.

Cold fear washed over her as smoke curled around the corner of the door. Callie grabbed the notebook and ran from the room toward the house's front door. Before she could reach it, another firebomb crashed through the window to the right of the door. A trail of flames fanned across the entry as a combustible liquid spread across the floor. Another bomb slammed through the window to the left of the door. With a loud whooshing sound a giant wall of fire rose to cut off her exit.

She clutched the notebook to her chest and stared in horror as she realized her escape routes had both been cut off. It only took her a moment to remember what Uncle Dan had taught her years ago when she'd come to live with him.

Holding tightly to the notebook, she dashed up the staircase into her room. She raised the window and stepped out onto the roof of the garage that joined the house at a ninety-degree angle. Uncle Dan, always mindful of her safety, had assigned her this bedroom so she would have an easy escape route in case of a fire on the ground floor.

Callie climbed out the window onto the roof and ran to the end where she shimmied down the gutter drainpipe at the corner of the garage. When she was on the ground, she ran to the back of the yard before she stopped and stared at the house now engulfed in flames.

Tears ran down her face as she pulled her cell phone from her pocket and dialed 911. "Nine-one-one," the operator's voice answered. "What is your emergency?"

"My house is on fire!" she screamed.

"Are you at 1901 Willow Springs Road?"

"Yes."

"Help is already on the way. Someone called it in."

In the distance she could hear the sirens, and she relaxed. "Thank you. I hear them. They're almost here."

Callie disconnected the call and stared at the house where she'd grown up being devoured by flames. Someone was determined to make Uncle Dan suffer. First they'd shot him, then tried to kill him in the Critical Care Unit, and now they'd burned his house down. What more could they do to him?

Her eyes grew wide as the truth hit her like a bolt of lightning. Uncle Dan hadn't been home, and they knew it. They hadn't come with the intention of hurting him. She was the one they were after. She could identify the person who'd tried to kill her uncle, and someone didn't intend for that to happen.

What more could they do to Dan Lattimer? They could kill his niece.

Seth slammed on the brakes a block away from Dan's house and jumped from the car. Fire trucks and police cars blocked the middle of the street, and he zigzagged through the obstacle course they created as he raced toward the burning house.

He stumbled when his foot struck a fire hose,

slamming him against the side of a hook and ladder fire truck parked next to the curb. Taking a deep breath, he pushed back to his feet and ran toward Dan's front yard.

Smoke poured from the burning building, and he stopped in the driveway of the house next door to survey the scene. In spite of the valiant efforts the Memphis firemen were waging, it was evident there was no way this house could be saved. At that moment the roof gave way and crashed to the ground.

Seth scanned the gathered crowd, but he couldn't spot Callie anywhere. Captain Wilson stood in a group of firefighters a few feet away, and he moved over to them. The captain acknowledged his arrival with a nod. "Can you believe this?" he said.

Seth shook his head. "How much more is going to happen to Dan and Callie tonight?"

The captain exhaled a deep breath. "I don't know. This is the busiest night we've had in a long time, and a lot of what's happened has centered on Dan."

"I know." Seth glanced around the bystanders. "Where is Callie? I don't see her anywhere."

Captain Wilson pointed toward his cruiser, which sat about halfway down the block. "She's in my car. Of course she was wearing her robe and pajamas and wasn't able to save any of her clothes. I told her to sit in there until we could figure out what to do."

"I'll go check on her. Maybe I can help."

Captain Wilson nodded. "Thanks."

Seth jogged down the street and stopped at the squad car parked there. He opened the front door and leaned in on the driver's side. Callie sat huddled against the front passenger side door, her head resting against the back of the seat.

"Callie, are you all right?"

She opened her eyes and sat up straighter. "Seth, what are you doing here? You should be home getting some rest."

He shook his head, climbed in the car and closed the door. "Captain Wilson called me when he got here, and I rushed right over. I wanted to check on you. How did you get out of the house?"

"The way Uncle Dan taught me when I was a child. Out my window, across the garage roof and down the drainpipe to the ground. I used to get tired of him making me practice, but now I'm glad he did. Otherwise I might be burned to a crisp in that house."

"Do you know how the fire started?"

She gave a wry chuckle. "Well, it wasn't faulty wiring, that's for sure."

He frowned. "What do you mean?"

"I'm sure the firemen have already discovered the smell of accelerant in the flames."

His eyes grew wide. "Are you saying the fire was set deliberately?"

"Yes."

For the next few minutes Seth listened as Callie related what had happened after he'd left her at the house. His heart sank when she described the flames racing across the entry and how she'd had to leap over some of them to get to the staircase. When she'd finished, she directed a somber stare at him.

"I keep thinking about how Uncle Dan acted after he picked me up at the airport. It was as if he knew somebody was after him. Why else would he have tried to get me to stay at the Peabody Hotel rather than at home?"

Seth nodded. "The fact that he said he needed to tell me something makes me think he probably had gotten some new information, something that might lead to solving this case. That would mean the shooting attempt was a way to keep him from ever revealing what he'd found out."

"Yes, but Uncle Dan didn't die."

"And you foiled the second attempt on his life."

Callie let out a long breath. "And now somebody knows I can identify the man who tried to kill Uncle Dan tonight. They want to shut me up for good, too. If I hadn't escaped the burning house, I'd be dead right now."

Seth raked his hand through his hair and he gritted his teeth. "This is my fault. I should never have left you alone. How could I ever face Dan again if I let anything happen to you?"

Callie reached over and placed her hand on his arm. "None of this is your fault, Seth. I should have known I'd be in danger after seeing the scar and tattoo on that man in Uncle Dan's room. But I have to admit, I'm glad I was able to find this before they torched the house."

He glanced at the notebook that sat in her lap. "You found Dan's notebook."

"Yes. Have you ever looked at it?"

"Yes. He showed it to me several times. He would be down in the dumps for days after finding out that his latest lead had gone nowhere. Sometimes I'd go over to his house, and he'd have it open to the woman's picture. I think he spent a lot of time looking at it and wishing she could tell him her secrets. But of course she couldn't."

"I'm glad I was able to save this. Maybe we can look through it tomorrow. There are several things I want to ask you about, but I'm too tired tonight." She stifled a yawn. "I couldn't go to sleep earlier, but I feel like I could now. The only problem is I have nowhere to sleep—not to mention no clothes and no money. My wallet burned in the fire. I have no idea where I'm going to stay."

"I do. You're going home with me. My sister's room is empty since she got married, and my mother and I would be happy to have you stay with us while you're in Memphis."

Her eyes grew wide. "I don't know if that's a good idea. Your mother probably hates me because of what happened between us, and I'm sure it would make you feel uncomfortable to have me in the house, too."

His face grew warm, but he tried to laugh. "I thought we had this settled. Our relationship was over a long time ago. I accepted that and so did my mother. Besides, with all Mom's activities, she's gone quite a bit."

Callie smiled. "So she's still trying to enjoy life to the fullest."

"Yeah. I never know what to expect next from her. I don't know if she'll be volunteering at one of the hospitals, going on a mission trip to Ecuador or off on a camping trip with her friends to the Smokies."

"I always liked her. Are you sure she won't mind my staying there for a few days?"

"She'll be happy to have you. So, which will

it be? I can pay for a hotel room or offer you the hospitality of the Dawtry household."

She studied him a moment before she smiled. "Thank you, Seth. It's easy to say we can let the past go, but it's really hard to do. I know you're only doing this because you promised Uncle Dan you'd take care of me, but I appreciate it."

He bit down on his lip and pulled his cell phone from his pocket. "I'll call Captain Wilson and tell him I'm taking you to my mother's house. I don't think there's any reason for you to stay around here any longer."

A few minutes later with the message delivered to the captain, the two of them walked back to Seth's car. He opened the passenger door for Callie and held it for her to climb inside. Before she did, she turned her head and stared over her shoulder at the still-burning fire. He heard a little sob in her throat before she ducked her head and got in.

When he slid behind the steering wheel, he glanced at her. She stared straight ahead through the windshield for a moment before she swiveled in her seat and faced him.

"I've always loved my uncle, but tonight when he was almost taken from me twice, I realized how thankful I should have been all these years for a man who devoted his life to me. I feel so ashamed, Seth, for accepting everything he did for me without letting him know how thankful I was for him."

"You shouldn't. Dan wouldn't want that."

"He wouldn't, because that's the kind of person he is. How many people are there who would spend all those years raising their niece or looking for the elusive answers to the identity of a murder victim?"

Seth rubbed the back of his neck and chuckled. "Not many, but then Dan's not like other people."

"He's not. And one thing about him that I tried to ignore but shouldn't have is that he was always a cop at heart, just like my dad." She sighed. "I've been thinking about what Anthony said about me being able to stand up to the bad guys like my father and uncle did."

"Why have you thought about that?"

"Because I never thought my temperament was anything like my father's or Uncle Dan's. I'm a lot like my mother. She was a very quiet woman. She never forced herself on anyone, and she was quick to ignore things people did to hurt her. Up to a certain point, that is. She would let harsh words or insults go for a while, but then she reached her breaking point. When that happened, I pitied the person she focused her anger on. It was like a dam broke, and all her pent-up emotions poured out."

"And you say you're like that, too?" Seth asked.

She nodded. "Maybe not as much as she was, but to some extent. Not many hours ago I flew into Memphis ready to go on a Hawaiian vacation with my uncle, who was about to retire. Within minutes, we were shot at, trapped in a wrecked vehicle and transported in an ambulance. My uncle then endured extensive surgery, was hooked up to life-saving machines and then nearly smothered by an assailant. That was quite enough, but someone wasn't through. He then attempted to murder me and burned down our house in the process, leaving Uncle Dan with no worldly possessions left. I think that's quite enough to exceed my breaking point, too."

Seth frowned. "I don't understand what you're saying, Callie."

She took a deep breath. "I'm saying that because I was there, I'm now on their list, too. Somebody tried to kill me in the wreck and then in the house—not to mention Scarface nearly shooting me before the marshal interrupted." She gritted her teeth and glared at him. "No way am I going to let these people get away with all they've done to my family. Whoever is behind all this has to be stopped. We need to find out who these people are and why they want to kill Uncle Dan and now me. And in finding them, we just might be able to discover Hope's identity and why someone doesn't want it revealed."

Seth stared at her in disbelief. "Are you saying you want to track down whoever's done these things to you and Dan?" He chuckled and shook his head. "Callie, you're a college professor. You know nothing about police work."

She nodded. "I know that, but I'm smart, Seth. And I'm determined. I can figure things out, and you understand how to investigate. I think we'd make a good team."

"I don't know, Callie. This is too dangerous for you to get involved in."

"I'm already involved, Seth. Somebody welcomed me into this case when he pointed a gun at the car I was riding in. I want to know who it was and why he did it. I think the only way to find out who that was is to first find out who Hope was and how she ended up in the Mississippi River."

He stared at her for a moment before he smiled. "Maybe you're right. I'd sure like to solve Dan's case. It can't hurt to give it a try. But first, let's try to get a few hours' sleep before we make any decision on this."

She buckled her seat belt and smiled. "That sounds good. I just hope I'm able to sleep after facing your mother for the first time since we broke up. I don't imagine she's going to be happy to see me on her doorstep."

Seth started to protest his mother would welcome Callie into their home, but instead he shook his head. His mother loved her children, and she could be as ferocious as a mother bear in protecting her offspring.

Uncertain of what awaited them, Seth started the car and headed toward home.

FOUR

Seth unlocked the front door of his house and allowed Callie to step inside first. She walked into the entry hall, stopped and looked around. He wondered if she was remembering the last time she'd been here. It had been almost two years ago, and she had come for dinner. His mother and sister had excused themselves after they'd eaten because they knew Seth was planning on proposing.

He still remembered the white summer dress she was wearing that night and how beautiful she'd looked in the light from the candles. Every time she smiled at him, he would reach down and touch his coat pocket where the ring box rested to make sure it was still there.

After dinner he and Callie had gone into the den and settled on the couch. It was then she'd turned to him and told him she had decided to take the job at the University of Virginia and would be leaving town at the end of the week.

The news had been so completely unexpected he could only stare at her in disbelief.

"B-but Callie," he had finally managed to stammer, "I thought you were going to take the job at the University of Memphis. What made you change your mind?"

She'd had trouble meeting his gaze. "It's quite an honor to be hired at Virginia."

"I know. But I don't want you to go. I want you to stay here and marry me. Have you changed your mind about loving me?"

A sad look had flickered in her eyes. "No, I haven't changed my mind. I do love you, but I don't think it's going to work out for us. I'm still young, and I'm not ready for marriage and motherhood. I want to concentrate on my career. I can't do that if I'm married."

He'd frowned and shaken his head. "I would never keep you from following your dreams. In fact, I would help you any way I could, and I wouldn't push you to have children until you were ready."

"But I know how important having a family is to you. You want to be the kind of father that you never had, and you need to find somebody who wants the same things you do."

"I don't want anybody else. I want you. Please take the job at the University of Memphis and marry me." The words had rolled from his mouth like a plea.

She'd shaken her head. "The program at Virginia is one of the best in the country, and I want to teach there."

He'd grabbed her hands and scooted closer. "This is about more than just the school where you'll teach. Does it have anything to do with the fact that I'm a policeman?"

She'd tried to pull away from him, but he tightened his grip. "Please, Seth. Don't make this harder than it already is."

He'd struggled to think of something to say that would change her mind. "Is this about your father's death? If it is, you can't live the rest of your life afraid the same thing is going to happen to someone else you love."

She'd pulled from his grip and slowly risen to her feet. "I'm sorry, Seth. I'm convinced you could never be happy with me. I've made up my mind, and nothing's going to change it."

Without another word she'd turned and walked from his house and out of his life. He hadn't spoken with her again until he'd arrived at the scene of the accident and saw her standing behind the ambulance. Now she was in his house again, and he could hardly believe it. He had to keep reminding himself that he was doing this for Dan. As far as Callie was concerned, he couldn't wait for her to go back to Virginia.

He shook his head to clear it of thoughts of the past and stepped inside. A sound in the kitchen caught his attention, and he glanced up to see his mother standing in the door at the end of the hall. Her long gray hair was pulled up in a bun at the back of her head, and she wore the comfortable robe he'd given her last Christmas. Her eyebrows were arched, and she darted a quick glance from Seth to Callie.

She frowned and settled her gaze on Seth. "I thought you'd gone to bed after you got home from the hospital. I didn't hear you go out again."

"I didn't want to wake you when I left. I received a call that Dan's house was on fire. Callie barely escaped with her life."

His mother's eyes darkened, and she stepped forward and grasped Callie's hands in hers. "How awful for you, my dear. Were you burned or hurt anywhere?"

Callie shook her head. "No, I was able to get out by going out the window of my bedroom. But it was a terrifying experience." She glanced at Seth and cleared her throat. "I'm sure you're surprised to see me here, but Seth insisted I come home with him. I don't want to be any bother to you. I'll check into a hotel later today."

"You'll do nothing of the sort. We have an empty bedroom, and you're welcome to stay here as long as you need." His mother's gaze raked Callie, who still wore her gown and robe. "It looks like you'll need some help with clothes first. I'll go to the mall as soon as it opens and pick you up a few things until you can get what you want."

Tears sparkled in Callie's eyes. "Thank you, Mrs. Dawtry. I wasn't sure how you'd feel about having me stay. Especially after the last time I was here."

His mother put her arm around Callie. "That was a long time ago. I just hope your life has turned out the way you wanted." She gestured toward the kitchen. "I'm an early riser, and I already have a pot of coffee made, if you want some. With the night you've had, I imagine you're worn out. I'll fix you some breakfast, or I'll show you to the guest room if you'd like."

Callie rubbed her hand across her eyes. "I think I'd like to go to bed for a while if that's all right. Please don't go to any trouble for me."

"I won't, but if you need anything, please let me know."

Seth motioned to the stairs. "I'll show you to your room."

His mother shook her head. "I can do that.

You go have a cup of coffee. I'll come back down after I've gotten Callie settled."

She grabbed Callie by the arm and guided her upstairs before he had a chance to object. Seth watched them go before he walked into the kitchen, poured himself a cup of coffee and sat down at the kitchen table. He stared down into the murky depths of his cup for a few minutes until he heard his mother reenter the room. He looked up as she slipped into the chair across from him. A worried frown wrinkled her forehead.

"Are you all right, Seth?" she asked.

He nodded. "Sure. Why would you ask that?"

She glanced over her shoulder toward the hallway stairs and back at him. "The woman you wanted to marry has just come into our home again. I'm afraid her presence here is going to bring back bad memories for you."

He shook his head. "I got over Callie a long time ago. When I saw Dan tonight, I knew he wanted me to watch out for her. I couldn't very well leave her on the street after his house burned down. How would I ever face him again if I'd done that?"

His mother nodded. "I know."

Seth raked his hand through his hair and swallowed hard. "I have to admit I was worried about bringing her here. You were angry with Callie for a long time after she left town."

"I've prayed a lot about my feelings toward Callie, and God has helped me deal with them." She reached across the table and covered his hand with hers. "I just don't want to see you get hurt again."

He tried to laugh, but the sound stuck in his throat. "Don't worry, Mom. I'm not about to put myself in that situation again. Callie may have broken my heart once, but she's not going to get the chance to do it again."

His mother stared at him as if she didn't believe him. After a moment she shrugged. "If you say so."

He picked up his cup and drained the coffee in one gulp before he pushed to his feet. "I'm beat. I'm going to grab a few hours' sleep before I go back to the station."

His mother stood to clear the table. "You go on upstairs. I may not be back from the mall by the time you leave. If not, I'll see you later tonight."

He stopped at the kitchen door and turned to face her. "Won't you be home for dinner?"

"No, I'm going out to eat and to a movie with my church circle group, just like I told you yesterday. You and Callie are on your own for dinner."

He grinned. "And Callie thought her staying here might be inconvenient for you."

She laughed. "Not at all. I figure you two adults can take care of yourselves. I have a life of my own, you know."

He smiled. "I'm glad you have a life, Mom. I wouldn't want you sitting at home all the time."

Her features darkened, and she walked over to him, reaching up to stroke his cheek. "That's what I want for you, son. A life of your own. You're just beginning to start going out again. I don't want your being around Callie again to change that."

He leaned over and kissed her on the cheek. "I promise that won't happen, Mom."

She sighed and headed back to the table. "Then go on and get some sleep."

He left the room and headed up the stairs. When he arrived at the landing of the second floor, he stopped outside the closed door to the bedroom where Callie was sleeping. He stared at the door for a moment and thought about what his mother had said.

For some reason his final conversation two years ago with Callie had been running through his mind a lot lately, and he didn't understand why. The more he'd thought about it, he realized she had never really given him a reason for not marrying him. At the time he'd thought it was because of her policeman father's death—that she didn't want to run the risk of losing someone else she loved. Now he wasn't so sure. Maybe there had been another reason. If so, what could it have been?

Callie awoke with a start and sat up in bed. She'd been dreaming of the fire, and the flames were about to engulf her when she bolted upright. She wiped her hand across her perspiring brow and swung her feet over the side of the bed.

Her stomach growled, and she glanced at the clock on the bedside table. It was nearly noon, and she realized she hadn't eaten since lunch yesterday. She glanced around the room and spotted several shopping bags next to the closed bedroom door. Mrs. Dawtry must have made good on her promise to go to the mall for her.

Callie hurried over and pulled off the note that was stapled to the side of the bag. She smiled as she read Mrs. Dawtry's message.

I bought you several pairs of slacks, two tops, some underwear and some flip-flops. Since I had to guess at the sizes, I hope everything fits. Maybe this will tide you over until you can pick out what you'd really like to have.
—Mona Dawtry

Thirty minutes later Callie hurried downstairs and into the kitchen. She came to a stop at the sight of Seth sitting at the kitchen table with a sandwich and a glass of iced tea in front of him. His gaze traveled over her.

"I see you found the clothes Mom bought for you."

Callie nodded. "Yes, that was so kind of her. I'll repay her as soon as I can get to the bank and get some money."

He shook his head. "Don't worry about it. You have other things on your mind right now."

She slid into the chair across from him. "Have you heard from the hospital?"

"Yes. There's no change. The marshals are still guarding him."

She crossed her arms on the table and leaned forward. "What are you doing here? I thought you'd be at work."

"I went in for a while this morning, but I wanted to be here when you woke up so I could take you to the hospital." He glanced down at his sandwich. "Can I make you something to eat?"

She shook her head and stood up. "No, I'll do it. Then I would like to go to the hospital. Are you planning on working this afternoon?"

"No. Why?"

She sighed. "I hate to keep asking you for favors, but I need to see about getting my driver's license replaced. Could you take me to the testing center to see what I have to do?"

"I'd be glad to. But you don't have to worry about driving yourself around. Until we've caught whoever tried to kill you and Dan, I'm going to be sticking to you, anyway. I don't want you going anywhere alone."

The memory of everything she'd experienced the night before flooded into her mind, and she swallowed the fear that threatened to engulf her. "Thank you, Seth. I appreciate your doing this for me."

He stared at her for a moment before he answered. Then he took a deep breath. "Let's get one thing straight, Callie. I don't want you reading anything into this arrangement. I'm doing this because of Dan. I'd do anything for him. That's all there is to it."

She blinked back the tears that threatened to fill her eyes and tried to smile. "I understand, but I still appreciate it." She pushed to her feet. "Now I think I'll fix myself one of those sandwiches. Then we can go to the hospital."

When she sat back down at the table with her food, the hunger she'd felt when she'd first entered the kitchen had vanished. Seth kept his gaze downcast as he finished his lunch, and Callie tried to force herself to eat. The food tasted like sawdust in her mouth.

With his last bite swallowed, Seth picked up his iced tea and took a long drink before he directed his attention back to her. "I'll be in the den. When you're ready to go, let me know."

Before she could reply, he picked up his dishes, deposited them in the sink and walked from the room. Callie took a deep breath and tried to slow her racing heartbeat as she listened to his retreating footsteps.

She propped her elbows on the table and buried her face in her hands. Seth had been very thoughtful of her feelings last night, but in the light of day his attitude toward her had changed. It didn't surprise her, but it still hurt.

Until her uncle's condition had improved and his attacker was caught, all she could do was endure Seth's feelings toward her and hope he would never find out the real reason she had refused his proposal.

Seth had dreaded accompanying Callie on her shopping trip. He'd often shaken his head in sympathy at the men he spotted sitting around the mall waiting for their wife or girlfriend to finish. Now he found himself one of those he'd often pitied.

He tried to slump down on the store's sofa in the middle of the ladies' clothes department, but it was impossible to make himself invisible.

Until Callie was finished trying on clothes, he was destined to wait and endure the knowing stares from other men who happened to walk by.

He looked up as Callie emerged from the dressing room and stepped in front of a full-length mirror. She twisted and turned as she examined the outfit she wore. When she saw him watching her, she smiled.

"I appreciate your taking the time to drive me to the hospital and now to the mall. I know you'd rather be anywhere else but here. I really appreciate you bringing me."

"No problem," he said. "Glad to help."

She glanced back at her reflection once more before she disappeared into the fitting room. After a few minutes, he spied the handbags display on several counters against the far wall, and an idea struck him. His sister's birthday was a week away, and he'd heard her tell their mother she needed a new purse. Maybe he could find one while he waited for Callie.

Ten minutes later a salesperson finished ringing up his purchase and handed him his change. "I hope your sister enjoys her new purse," she said.

"I'm sure she will. She…"

Before he could finish the sentence, a shrill scream from the direction of the ladies' changing area pierced the air. Seth whirled, and instinct kicked in. He pulled his gun from its holster on his belt where his badge was displayed. "Call store security and have them lock the building down," he ordered the cashier. "Then call 911 for backup."

Without waiting for an answer, he charged toward the fitting room where he'd left Callie. "Police!" he yelled as he stopped at the doorway.

"Help!" The frantic cry made his blood run cold. It wasn't just the fear he could hear in the woman's voice—it was the fact that it wasn't *Callie's* voice. He couldn't hear her at all.

He peered around the door and spotted the salesclerk who'd been helping Callie on the floor with blood trickling down her face. Seth dropped to his knees beside her. "What happened?"

"A man," she gasped. "He came in here while I was helping the customer and knocked me down. Then he grabbed her by the arm and pulled her out. He had a gun to her head."

"Lie still," Seth ordered. "Help is on the way. I'm going after them."

He ran from the dressing room and glanced around. Salespeople and customers huddled in clumps around the room, but Callie and her abductor were nowhere to be seen. Then he spotted the exit sign over a door behind the cash register and ran toward it.

The door opened into a long hallway, and Seth recognized the direction it led. This was an entrance for employees from the parking garage. Whoever had Callie was trying to get to a car to escape.

Seth sprinted down the hall toward the far door and exited onto the lower level of the parking garage. Clutching his gun in front of him with both hands, he scanned the area for Callie. He didn't see her, but then a cry echoed through the garage.

The sound seemed to come from his right, past the row of parked cars that lined the side of the garage. He charged down the concrete surface toward the end of the row and rounded a curve that led to more parking spaces. Halfway down the parking section, he spotted a van with its side door pushed back. A man inside the van pulled on one of Callie's arms, and another stood behind her, holding her other arm twisted behind her back.

"Police!" he yelled. "Let the woman go."

The man behind Callie whirled and pointed his gun at Seth. Just as he fired, Callie screamed and shoved against him. Seth heard the bullet whiz by his head.

Seth lunged behind a parked car for cover and peered around the bumper. Even though Callie appeared to be putting up a good fight, it was evident she couldn't keep from being pushed into the van much longer. Afraid a bullet might hit her, Seth aimed at the back tire, and it exploded in a rush of air.

The second bullet ricocheted off the top of the van, and the man inside yelled a curse at him. Seth fired two more shots in rapid succession. The man inside the van released Callie and jumped to the ground. "Let's go," he yelled.

The other assailant knocked Callie to the ground, and the two of them ran to the half wall around the perimeter of the parking area. They jumped the barrier and disappeared.

Seth sprang to his feet and rushed to Callie. She was just pushing to her knees when he reached her. "Are you all right?"

She nodded. "Yes. See if you can get them."

Seth rushed to the wall and scanned the area outside the parking garage, but the men were nowhere in sight. They had either ducked into another store or an accomplice had been waiting outside with a separate getaway car to make sure they made it out okay.

He returned to Callie and pulled her to her feet. "Are you sure you're okay?"

She nodded. "Yes."

"What happened?"

"The salesclerk and I had just gone back to the dressing room when a man ran in and grabbed me. When the lady helping me tried to intervene, he hit her in the head with the butt of his gun."

"Did you recognize the man?"

Callie shook her head. "He had a ski mask on. He must have pulled it on right before he entered the fitting room, or someone would have noticed."

"Yeah. That would have stood out, all right, especially since it's summertime." His gaze raked Callie from head to foot. She had no apparent injuries. Except for being frightened, she appeared to have come through the incident quite well. "If you're sure you're up to it, we need to get back to the store. Security and the police should have everything in there under control now, but you'll need to give your statement."

Callie took a step before she stopped, her eyes wide. "I haven't asked about the clerk yet. Is she all right?"

"I think so. Let's go see."

As they walked toward the exit, Seth's heart thudded as guilt washed over him. How could he have been so careless and left Callie like that? It wouldn't happen again.

He glanced once more at the barrier the assailants had jumped. Somewhere out there were assassins determined to kill Callie. He didn't know who they were or why they wanted her dead, but he intended to find out. From now on, he wasn't going to let her out of his sight.

From her chair at the kitchen table Callie glanced out the window at the gathering night shadows. The memory of what had happened earlier today in the department store returned, and she shivered. She pressed her fingers to her temples and rubbed in small circles to fight off the looming headache. From the minute she'd arrived in Memphis her life had been turned upside down, and she didn't know how much more she could take.

Across the table Seth looked up, and their eyes met. He'd said very little while they ate, and she had found it difficult to carry on a conversation, too. "How are you?" he asked.

"I'm fine, Seth."

He raked his hand through his hair. "I'm so sorry for leaving you, Callie. I won't do that again."

"Seth, it wasn't your fault. If you'd been there, it could have been worse. Either one of us could have been shot. It all worked out in the end, so let's not talk about it anymore."

Instead of replying, he rose to his feet and began to clear away the containers of carry-out Chinese food they'd eaten. When he'd tossed them in the garbage can, he turned back to her and pointed to her uncle's notebook she'd brought downstairs before they began to eat. "There has to be something in this notebook to give us a clue to what Dan found out before you arrived in Memphis."

He sat back down, and Callie pushed the notebook over in front of him. "I've looked through it so many times and nothing stands out to me, but I agree. We're overlooking something."

Seth stared at the picture of the woman her uncle had named Hope and smiled. "Every time I look at this picture, I'm struck by how beautiful she was."

Callie nodded. "Yes, and I can see some resemblance to my mother in the shape of her mouth, though I think Uncle Dan may have exaggerated their similar features. Probably the locket with the little boy's picture in it is what touched his heart."

"I think you're right."

Callie stared at the picture a moment before she looked up at Seth. "Where is the necklace now?"

"It's part of the evidence and is in the box containing everything about this cold case."

"Was there anything unusual about it that would enable you to trace where it might have been made or sold?"

Seth shook his head. "No. It's just an inexpensive gold locket, the kind you see in stores all the time. Dan searched the internet for a long time, trying to find a source for similar ones, but it was no use. He finally decided that would never lead to anything."

"I see." Callie reached across and pulled the notebook in front of her. "There's something in the back I want to show you." She flipped through the pages until she found the sheet with the list of names on it. "Have you ever seen this before?"

Seth nodded as he scanned the page. "I saw it some time ago. This is a list of people who the police use as informants. Dan thought one of them might have heard something on the street that would help him. The last time I talked to him about it, though, it hadn't led to anything."

Callie pursed her lips and pointed to the name she had first noticed when she looked at the page. "What about Melvin Harris? Did Uncle Dan ever say anything about him? His name has a check mark beside it."

Seth frowned and stared at the name. "I told Dan that Melvin is an informant I've used for years ever since I started on the force. I remember when he wrote the name down, but I have no idea why he would have put a check beside it."

"Can you call him and ask him if he talked to Uncle Dan?"

Seth smiled and shook his head. "It doesn't work that way, Callie. I can't just call up an informant. He has to be very careful about making contact with me. It could mean his life if the wrong people thought he talked to the police about them."

Callie's eyebrows arched. "I never thought about that. How do you contact him?"

"Melvin lives on the south side of town. I drive through his neighborhood, and if he's on the street, he'll give me a signal to meet him. Then I wait for him at the spot where we usually meet."

Callie looked back at the check mark next to Melvin's name. "Uncle Dan must have had some reason for making that mark. Maybe we need to talk to Melvin and see if they'd met recently."

Seth scooted his chair back from the table and shook his head. "Wait a minute! After what happened today, what makes you think I'd agree to take you with me to talk to a police informant? I'm not letting you put yourself in danger again."

She stood up and braced her hands on the table before she leaned toward him. "With all that's happened to me since I've been in Memphis, I think I have the right to help uncover what's going on. We need to find out who these people are before they come back and finish what they started out to do—kill Uncle Dan and me. Please don't leave me out of finding them."

He stared at her for a moment before he pushed to his feet. "Okay. I'll let you go with me to find Melvin, but that's as much as I'm willing to compromise. Besides, finding Melvin may not be as easy as you think. Sometimes he disappears for days, and I'm unable to locate him."

"I understand. If we don't find him, we can keep going back until we do. At least we'll be doing something to find out who's behind all that's happened."

Seth stared at her for a moment before he sighed. "I hope we can. Nothing would please me more than to have all this brought to an end." He glanced at his watch. "Now if you'll excuse me, I need to get some sleep. I have to go into the office in the morning, but I've made arrangements for a police officer to watch the house while I'm gone. He'll be out front in his car until I come back after lunch. Then I'll take you to the hospital before we go on the hunt for Melvin."

"Thank you, Seth. I'll see you then."

He gave a curt nod and walked from the room. Callie dropped back down in her chair, propped her elbows on the table and covered her eyes with her hands. His words that noth-

FIVE

The next afternoon Seth drove his car slowly up and down the streets of south Memphis. Callie sat beside him. She hadn't said a word since they'd left the hospital after checking on Dan. The news didn't seem to change any. Dan hadn't regained consciousness, but he was still holding his own. Seth supposed they should be thankful Dan was still alive, but gratitude proved harder every time he entered the Critical Care Unit to see his friend clinging to life by a thread.

He glanced at Callie out of the corner of his eye. She appeared hopeful that if they were able to find Melvin he would have some answers for them. He understood how badly she wanted the attacker caught, but he suspected there was more to her thinking than she'd shared with him.

Clearly, she couldn't wait to be away from him and out of the house he shared with his mother.

If things worked out the way she hoped,

maybe he could make quick work of finding the culprit of the attacks, solving the decades-old missing-person case and leaving her and her uncle free of all danger. Then she could go back to living the life she'd chosen.

"Where do you usually see him?" Callie's words cut through the silence in the car.

He darted a glance at her before he directed his attention back to the street ahead. "I never know. It may be on a street corner, under a light pole or playing basketball on the playground at the school down the street. If I don't see him within the next few minutes, I need to leave. There are always eyes watching who comes into this neighborhood, and I don't want my car to draw any attention."

Seth guided the car around the corner and sucked in his breath at the sight of Melvin walking up the sidewalk toward them. As they drove past, Melvin tucked his chin to his chest, stuck his hands in the pockets of the baggy shorts he was wearing and hunched his shoulders. He'd given the signal he wanted to talk with Seth.

Seth didn't slow the car but gave a slight nod. He watched Melvin in the rearview mirror as he drove on down the street. Beside him, Callie, oblivious to the fact that he had just made contact with his informant, stared out the window. When he turned out of the neighborhood and drove toward the interstate that skirted the area, she swiveled in her seat and frowned at him. "Are you giving up already?"

Seth chuckled. "No. We passed him already. Melvin just gave me the sign that he would meet me at our usual place in an hour."

Her eyes grew wide. "I didn't see anybody. When did that happen?"

"I guess you were looking out the wrong window. We have an hour until we meet him, so I thought we could grab a cup of coffee while we're waiting."

"Why do we have to wait so long?"

"Because Melvin has to make sure no one follows him. This is our normal routine. We always follow it."

The flashing sign of a fast-food restaurant down the street caught his attention, and he pulled into the parking lot. As they walked toward the front door, he glanced over at her. A smile pulled at her lips.

"What is it?" he asked.

"I might have known you'd look for your favorite fast-food franchise. I think I ate my weight in hamburgers that summer we dated. Every time we went to a movie or a ball game, we had to end the evening at one of these restaurants. I think you must have been on a quest that summer to eat at every one in the city."

His face grew warm, and he grinned. "I'm sorry. Would you rather go somewhere else that doesn't bring up unpleasant memories?"

A surprised look flashed in her eyes. "I didn't say they were unpleasant memories, Seth. I'm glad we have some memories that don't bring pain."

He didn't know how to answer her, so he bit down on his lip and reached around her to open the door to the restaurant. She walked inside, and he followed her to the counter. After purchasing their coffee, they settled in a booth near the back of the room.

Seth sipped the hot liquid in his cup and let his gaze settle on Callie. He kept telling himself that he had to stay strong and not let her get under his skin again the way she had two years ago. He thought he'd been doing a good job of it until she'd hinted that some of the things they'd shared in their relationship had made her happy.

"So," he said and took a deep breath, "you don't regret everything about our time together?"

Her eyes grew wide. "Of course I don't. I know I left abruptly, and you didn't understand. I've always been sorry I hurt you, but I thought in time you'd come to see I wasn't right for you. I hope you've done that."

He nodded. "It was hard at first, but it got

better through time. Dan helped me through it. I don't know what I would have done without him."

"I know. He helped me, too." She traced her finger around the rim of her cup. "When I came back to Memphis this time, I meant to stay away from you, but now I realize that was a mistake. Both of us love Uncle Dan, and he loves us. He's had a hard time the past two years trying to walk the line between us without hurting anyone. I don't want that for him anymore. If he recovers, I think we need to do everything we can to put the past behind us and be friends for his sake. Then when I come home, there won't be any problems about you coming over to see us. We can truly be happy to see each other. Do you think we can do that?"

Seth stared at her for a moment before he answered. "I'd like to do that, Callie, but I don't know if I can unless we can base our friendship on truth."

"But our relationship has always been built on truth."

He cocked his head to one side and stared at her. "Really? Then maybe it's time you told me the truth about why you turned down my proposal."

Her face turned pale, and her mouth gaped

open. "B-but I t-told you. I wanted to pursue my career in Virginia."

"I know what you told me. You also led me to believe that it was because I was a policeman, and your father was killed in the line of duty. But after two years of thinking about it, I don't buy either one of those excuses. When are you going to break down and tell me what really made you decide not to marry me?"

Her lips trembled, and tears gathered in the corners of her eyes. "Seth, I'm sorry if you can't accept my reasons, but…"

He held up his hand. "You're wrong. I have accepted the fact that it ended with us two years ago. I just want to know why. I don't think it could have been another guy because Dan says you aren't involved with anyone. It just makes no sense."

She straightened in her seat, and a tear slid down her cheek. "Again, I'm sorry, but there's nothing else I can tell you other than that I didn't think we were right for each other. Please drop this and do what I asked. Just be my friend. With my only relative near death, I need a friend, and you're the only one I can turn to. I need your friendship, Seth."

He exhaled a deep breath and leaned against the back of the booth. Why had he brought this up today? He'd always suspected there was some hidden reason Callie had run away from him, but she was determined not to tell him what it was.

Perhaps he needed to forget about her reasons and accept the friendship she was offering now. He knew nothing would make Dan happier than to know that the two people he loved most in the world had gotten past the anger of the past. He could do that, if not for himself then for Dan.

He nodded. "All right, Callie. Whatever your reasons, you've made it clear you're not going to share them with me. But I agree that we owe it to Dan to try and rebuild some kind of friendship. I'll try if you will."

She smiled and reached across the table to grasp his hand. "Thank you, Seth. I promise I'll try, too."

He glanced down at her hand resting on his and threaded his fingers through hers. For the first time in two years he felt a twinge of peace radiating through his soul like a light trying to pierce the darkness in a tunnel. It felt good to be here with Callie. Now if the doctors could get Dan out of the woods and he could protect Callie, maybe the three of them could once again share the good times they'd had in the past. He hoped so.

Seth let his gaze drift down the alley that served as his appointed meeting place with Melvin. It ran behind the row of small businesses that fronted a busy street in south Memphis. He pulled to a stop behind a Laundromat and glanced over at Callie. "Do you want to come with me or wait in the car?"

"I'd rather come with you if that's all right. Will he be willing to talk with you with me present?"

"I don't know, but I guess we'll find out."

He'd barely finished speaking when Melvin stepped out the back door of the Laundromat and stopped in front of his car. His gaze settled on Callie as they climbed from the vehicle. "What's this, man? How come you go bringing a woman down here with you?"

Seth walked around the front of the car, leaned back against the fender and crossed his arms. "You don't have to worry about her, Melvin. She's all right. In fact, she's the niece of a man maybe you've heard about—Judge Dan Lattimer."

At the mention of Dan's name, Melvin's eyes grew wide. "Why you coming 'round here asking me about that judge?"

Seth shrugged. "Maybe because your name showed up in some of his files. I need to know if you've talked to him lately."

Melvin shot an angry glance at Callie. "If

you want to know all that bad, why don't you just ask him?"

Seth was relieved to see that Callie didn't rise to the bait, leaving the talking to him. "Because he's not able to talk right now. It seems somebody shot him night before last. You know anything about that?"

Melvin's eyes widened, and his Adam's apple bobbed up and down. "Oh, no. I warned him to watch his back."

Callie sucked in her breath, and Seth shot her a look that he hoped convinced her to remain quiet and let him handle this. He turned his attention back to Melvin. "You did? Then it seems you have some information for me."

Melvin glanced at Callie once more before he nodded. "Yeah, but you know how these things work."

"I do. You give me something I want, and I help you out with something you want."

"That's right, and I got me a need."

Seth narrowed his eyes and frowned. "I figured you did. What is it?"

Melvin licked his lips and took a step closer to Seth. "My check don't come until the end of the month, and I'm running a little short. How about helping me out?"

Seth cocked an eyebrow. "What do you need money for?"

"I need milk and diapers for my baby."

Seth stroked his chin. "For your baby? Not for that habit of yours?"

Melvin straightened his shoulders and glared at Seth. "I told you. I quit fooling around with that stuff."

"I'm glad to hear it, Melvin, and I'm sorry you're running short on milk and diapers. I tell you what I'll do. I'll stop by Mr. Parson's store and leave some money on an account for your wife to spend, but I'm going to tell him she can only use it for milk, diapers or baby food. Understand?"

Melvin nodded. "Yeah, man. I get it. You don't have to worry. I'm gonna see my son is taken care of."

"Good. Now tell me, how do you know Judge Lattimer?"

Melvin looked over his shoulder and inched closer to Seth. "Everybody around here knows him. When folks wanted a neighborhood center built for their kids, Judge Lattimer was one of the first to donate money, and he gave a lot of it. But that's not all. After it was built, he started volunteering there. He's helped keep a lot of kids out of trouble."

Seth nodded. "Yeah, I know."

"He coaches my little brother's basketball team. I know it's because of the judge that he's been able to keep away from the gangs and stay out of trouble. So," Melvin continued, "when word on the street said somebody had put out a hit on him, I let him know."

"How did you do that?"

"I went down to the center one day last week, and I told him. He thanked me and said he'd be careful. But I guess they got to him anyway. How is he?"

Seth glanced at Callie, who still hadn't spoken. "He's in the hospital, but we're hoping he makes it."

Melvin nodded. "I sure hope he does."

"Do you know who put out the hit on Dan?"

"No, but I know who the shooter was. It was Carlos Allen."

Seth's breath hitched in his throat at the mention of the name he'd heard off and on ever since he'd joined the police force. Carlos had been in and out of trouble in Memphis for years, but it had been mostly for gang activities. If he was now hiring out as a hit man, he must have acquired a new set of skills and spread his wings in the criminal community.

"I know him. When I joined the police force, he was a gang member. I haven't heard much from him lately, though. I thought maybe he'd left town."

Melvin shook his head. "No, he's still around.

Not into the gang scene so much anymore. He's moved up in the world."

Seth thought for a moment before he asked the next question. "Any idea where I might find him?"

"Yeah, one of two places. I heard he's been doing a lot of community service time down at the Midtown Mission."

"That's interesting," Seth said. "And where else might I find him?"

"At Sam's Bar and Grill over on Highway 61." Melvin glanced over his shoulder. "If that's all, I need to get out of here. I don't want nobody catching me talking to a cop. That ain't healthy in this neighborhood."

Seth held up his hand to stop Melvin from leaving. "One more thing, Melvin. Did you tell Judge Lattimer where he might be able to find Carlos?"

"Yeah." He glanced over his shoulder. "I've told you all I know. Now I need to go."

"Okay, Melvin. I appreciate your help, and I'll leave that money at Mr. Parson's store. Take care of the baby. Being a father is a big responsibility. You need to make sure you do everything you can to give your son a good life."

Melvin didn't say anything, just gave him one last look before he turned and walked away. When he'd rounded the corner and disappeared from view, Callie stepped forward. "Do you think he was telling the truth?"

"He's never lied to me before, and he's right about Dan being respected in this neighborhood. At least now I have a name to start with. I haven't thought of Carlos Allen in a long time, but being a hit man for somebody is the sort of thing he'd like. Besides that, the gang he belonged to made their members get a star tattooed on their necks. That goes along with the description you gave of Dan's attacker at the hospital."

Callie's mouth curled into a large smile. "Then all we have to do is go to this bar and grill and wait for him. Then you can arrest him."

Seth shook his head and waved his hands in dismissal. "*We* are not going to the bar. I will go with police backup. *You* are not going near that place."

Her eyes turned dark with anger. "You can't do that. I thought we were going to work on this case together."

"We are going to work together to find out who Hope is, but the attempts on your and Dan's lives are another matter. That is police business that would put you directly in harm's way. I'm not about to take you into the middle of a police stakeout."

"But I won't let you do this. I'll…"

"You won't do anything," he interrupted. "I'm

going to take you back to my house and get a police officer stationed outside to guard you, then I'm going to headquarters and set up a stakeout for tonight. I'll let you know when I get home if anything happened or not."

Her face flamed with anger. "When you get home?"

He gritted his teeth and clenched his hands at his sides. "Yes. You're not going with me. Now let's get out of here before somebody comes by and recognizes me."

She started to say something else, but after a moment she whirled around and stormed toward the car. She climbed inside and slammed the door closed. Seth hesitated a moment and stared at her through the windshield, but she refused to look him in the eye.

Her anger was understandable. She wanted the person caught who had tried to kill her and her uncle. He wanted that, too, but not at the expense of putting her life in danger again. Carlos Allen had been on his way to a lifetime career in crime when Seth had first encountered him. It surprised him to think that somehow he had managed to stay under the radar all these years, enough to keep out of jail. Being picked for hit jobs wasn't something that went to inexperienced guys, so he must have been active in criminal circles all this time.

If so, why hadn't he surfaced before now? Finding out what he'd been doing for the past few years was just one more secret to be unraveled. Seth hoped the stakeout he planned for tonight would lead to many questions being answered.

Callie took a bite of the cheeseburger on her plate, washed it down with a sip of her soft drink and glanced around the room. The proprietor, whose name tag identified him as Sam, had frowned when she'd first walked in. With its high-carb, high-fat menu, the single women who came in here probably weren't his favorite customers, but he had lightened up some when she ordered a cheeseburger and fries. Lucky for her this place was a grill as well as a bar. She'd never been a drinker and wouldn't have known what to say if all Sam served was alcohol.

Now she sat in the back booth and kept a watch on every patron who walked in the door of Sam's Bar and Grill. So far most of those who had entered didn't come close to matching what she remembered about Carlos's size and appearance. Even if she was able to recognize him, she had no idea what she would do. She couldn't walk up to him and accuse him of trying to kill her.

But then, what if he recognized her? Her

heart lurched at the thought. Maybe coming here hadn't been such a good idea after all. She would never have done it if Seth had just given in and let her accompany him, maybe sit in a police car around the corner. When he'd refused, she'd become so angry that she was determined she was going to be at Sam's Bar and Grill to see firsthand what went down on a police sting operation.

She'd no sooner completed the thought than the door opened, and Seth walked inside. As his gaze drifted over the room, she slid down in the booth in hopes he wouldn't see her, but this wasn't her lucky day.

His eyes locked on her, and his mouth dropped open in surprise. Callie squirmed in her seat as his lips thinned into an angry expression, and his eyes darkened. With fists clenched at his side, he strode across the room and stopped at her booth.

"What are you doing here?" he demanded.

She straightened in her seat and took a deep breath to calm her racing heart. "I'm having dinner. Want to join me?"

He flattened his palms on the table and leaned closer to glare at her. "Don't try to be funny with me. I told you not to come."

She scooted toward the wall of the booth in

an effort to distance herself from him. "I wanted to be here in case anything happened."

He slid into the seat beside her. "I was thinking of your safety when I said I didn't want you here."

Callie realized he had blocked her escape. She might as well try to make the best of the situation. She sighed. "I know you were, Seth, and I appreciate it. I thought if Carlos did show up I might be able to identify him. After all, I did get a look at the tattoo on his neck and the scar on his face. You can't arrest him without evidence and I'm your only witness—other than Melvin, who wouldn't be willing to testify, right?"

Seth stared at her for a moment before he let out a deep breath. "How did you get away from my mother to come here?"

Her face warmed, and she reached for her soft drink. "When she came home, she told me she had just talked to you. She said it was just going to be the two of us for dinner because you were getting ready to leave on a stakeout. I told her that I had somewhere else I needed to be, and that I'd called a cab so she didn't need to drive me. The cab pulled up just then, so she didn't have time to ask any questions. I came down here in hopes I'd arrive first. And I did."

"Yes, you did." He raked his hand through

his hair. "Where is the officer who was in front of the house?"

"He's outside in his car. I told him I wouldn't be here long."

"Did you tell him this was a stakeout?"

"Well, no, but..."

"You should have told him, Callie." Seth frowned and shook his head. "He has to take you home now."

She shook her head. "No, please let me stay."

"This is no place..."

Before he could finish the sentence, the front door opened, and a man ambled in. Seth straightened in his seat and spoke into his lapel mike. "Suspect just entered the premises. He's approaching the bar. Be on alert. I'm going to intercept him now."

Callie stared at the man who strolled across the room as if he didn't have a care in the world. She frowned and studied his features. He wasn't as young as she'd expected. Maybe forty-five years old. But she couldn't make out the tattoo from where she was sitting. The build and coloring seemed right...but she couldn't be sure. Beside her Seth started to move, and she grabbed his arm.

"Seth, wait."

He glanced at her hand on his arm and then up at her. "Don't worry. There are police officers outside. If all goes well, we should have our suspect in custody in a few minutes. If he draws a gun, try to stay out of the line of fire."

Fear flowed through her, but she nodded as Seth pushed to his feet. She reached out to him once more. "Be careful."

He turned back to her, and a smile curled his lip. "I will. Now wait here for me."

She nodded as he started to turn toward the bar, not realizing someone was directly behind him. She tried to warn him, but nothing came out of her mouth. As if in slow motion, he turned, took a step and plowed into a waitress carrying a tray stacked high with dirty dishes. She tried to rebalance the tray, but it was no use.

Patrons spun around in their booths and on their bar stools as the crash of shattering plates and glasses cut through the quiet of the room. Carlos Allen had just stopped on his way to the bar. He whirled at the noise and fastened his gaze on Seth.

Recognition lit his face. With a snarl he reached underneath his shirt and pulled a gun out. He aimed at Seth, who dove for cover at the end of the bar. In an instant Seth had his back pressed against the end of the bar and his gun out of its holster. "Police!" he yelled. "Put your weapon down, Carlos."

Several patrons at the bar jumped up off their

stools and leaped to the floor on the other side of the bar. A woman at a table screamed, and the man she was with pulled her to the floor. Callie cringed in the booth, unable to move, until Carlos took a sideways step that gave him a clear view of Seth—just before Carlos cocked the trigger and grinned.

Callie grabbed the bottle of ketchup on the table, jumped to her feet and hurled it at Carlos before he could fire. The bottle hit him in the chest, and he growled. He whirled, and his eyes grew wide when he spotted Callie standing next to the booth. "You!" he yelled and pointed the gun at Callie.

"Callie!" She heard the panic in Seth's voice. Then a force like being tackled by a linebacker slammed into her, and she landed in the seat of the booth with Seth shielding her body. A bullet whizzed over the top of the booth and struck the far wall.

She waited for the second shot, but all she heard was the banging of the front door. In the next moment Seth jumped to a standing position, and she could hear him speaking into his lapel mike.

"Suspect armed and on his way out the front door."

Callie wriggled upright from the booth seat, but her heart was beating so fast she didn't think she could get to her feet. Seth glanced at the door, then back at her. "Are you all right?"

"I—I think so."

"I've got to go after Carlos. Stay here until I get back."

Without waiting for an answer, he ran toward the door. He'd just reached out to open it when gunfire from outside split the air. He jerked the door open and ducked as a bullet shattered the door frame above his head.

He only hesitated a moment before he ran outside, leaving Callie to wonder what had happened on the sidewalk in front of the bar. Several more gunshots split the night air before silence descended. Several patrons in the bar rose from where they'd tried to seek cover. She jumped to her feet and debated what she should do.

Guilt welled up in her and sucked the breath from her body. What had happened outside? Had her presence tonight compromised Seth's stakeout? Was he lying on the sidewalk injured or even worse, dead because of her? She had to find out. Stifling a sob, she ran to the door.

SIX

The scene on the sidewalk outside the bar and grill reminded Callie of something from the movies. Police cars, their lights flashing, sat in the street, and policemen in bulletproof vests stood around the prone figure of Carlos Allen, who lay in a pool of blood. She knew right away he was dead.

Seth, still holding his gun, stared down at the body as if he couldn't believe what had just happened. He looked up at the police lieutenant standing next to him. "Lieutenant Weaver, I thought I made it clear in our briefing that I wanted him taken alive. What happened?"

The officer hurried to say, "I know you did, Detective. When he came out of the bar, we yelled at him to put down his gun, but he raised it as if he was going to fire. There was nothing we could do once he made the threat. We had to return fire."

Seth shook his head. "*Return* fire? Did he actually fire the gun, or did he only raise it?"

The muscle in Weaver's jaw flexed, and he frowned at Seth. "I don't know. Everything happened so fast. Are you saying that we acted too soon?"

"I'm saying that you knew I was on my way out of the bar, and all of you were well covered. Who fired the first shot?"

"There was so much happening at once, it was hard to tell where the shot came from."

Seth frowned. "So you're telling me you really don't know what happened?"

The lieutenant's face turned red, and he glared at Seth. "I'll have you know—"

Before he could finish his sentence, another police car pulled up to the curb and Anthony Wilson climbed out. Callie breathed a sigh of relief. Maybe he could calm the confrontation between Seth and the officer.

Anthony stepped up on the sidewalk and glanced down at the body. "What happened here?"

Before Seth could speak, Weaver blurted out his response. "I had my men out here on backup. When this guy ran out of the bar, Detective Dawtry notified us he was armed. We yelled for him to lay down his weapon, but he raised it instead, and my officers fired. Now the detective is blaming us for being too quick to react. I might expect this from the media, but not from a member of the force."

Seth shook his head. "I'm not blaming him. I'm just frustrated." Seth pointed to Carlos's body. "This is the guy who tried to kill Dan. Now that he's dead, we may never know who hired him."

Anthony took a step so that he was almost between the two of them and held up a hand. "Blaming each other is not going to help any. We've all worked stakeouts enough to know that the unexpected can happen. I'm sorry this man's dead, especially if he knew something about the attack on Dan. However, we can't fight among ourselves. Let's get this scene processed and the body out of here."

Weaver bit down on his lip, gave a slight nod and glared at Seth once more before he turned and walked to where a group of officers stood. Anthony put a hand on Seth's shoulder. "You've overreacted here, Seth. If you'd been outside, you might have done the same thing. Marty Weaver is a well-respected officer. He's been honored several times for bravery beyond the call of duty, and you as much as called him incompetent tonight. I'm afraid your relationship with Dan is clouding your judgment."

Seth shook his head. "No, it's not, Anthony. I

promise you, I'm thinking clearly. I just thought if we could bring Carlos in, we could find out who wanted to kill Dan."

"We will find out, Seth, but not with this lead. You'll have to find another one." He looked over Seth's shoulder and when he saw Callie, his eyes grew wide. "Callie, what are you doing here?"

Callie eased forward. "I thought I might be able to identify Carlos as the man who tried to kill Uncle Dan in the hospital."

He turned a disbelieving stare on Seth. "You let her come on a police stakeout?"

Before he could answer, Callie rushed forward. "No, Anthony. It wasn't that way at all. In fact, Seth told me not to come, but I came anyway. I got here before he did and was waiting inside when he arrived."

"Do you know how dangerous that was, Callie?" Anthony asked. "How could I have ever faced Dan again if you'd been hurt?"

Tears pooled in her eyes, and she glanced from Anthony to Seth. "I know, and I'm really sorry. I won't interfere again. I promise."

Anthony swallowed and shook his head. "See that you don't. Now, I think you need to go home. Seth, can you take her? I'll stay here until Lieutenant Weaver and his men get through and the crime scene guys get things cleaned up."

Seth nodded. "Yes, sir. I'll do that. And thank

you, sir, for talking with me. I'll apologize to
Lieutenant Weaver tomorrow." He turned to
stare at Callie. "And about that police officer
you led here…"

She stared down at her feet and nodded. "I
know. I owe him an apology, too. I'll go talk
with him now."

Ten minutes later, after making her apology,
Callie took a deep breath and walked back to
where Seth waited. Without speaking, he took
her by the arm and propelled her around the corner and down the street to where he had parked
his car. From time to time she looked up at him
and saw him chewing on his bottom lip. She
dreaded what he would say once they were in
the car.

When they were both seated in the car, she
waited for him to speak but he sat there clutching the steering wheel. After a moment Callie
could contain herself no longer. "Seth, I'm sorry
I made such a mess of things today."

He turned to her, and a surprised look flashed
on his face. "You think you made a mess of
things?"

"Yes. If I hadn't been so concerned to get my
own way, I would have stayed home like you
asked. Then maybe you could have taken Carlos into custody. As it was, I proved to be a dis-
traction. I'm so sorry."

He sighed and rubbed his hands across his eyes. "It wasn't you, Callie. If I hadn't been so clumsy and run into that waitress, we might have Carlos right now." His gaze raked over her. "I hope I didn't hurt you when I tackled you."

She smiled and reassured him, "I may be sore tomorrow, but I'm glad you did it. I didn't know you could move so fast."

He grinned. "I figured it was the least I could do. After all, if you hadn't tried to stop the bad guy with a ketchup bottle, I might be on my way to the hospital right now or the morgue."

Callie shuddered at the thought. "Don't say that. I can't stand to think about it."

The teasing look he'd had on his face a few minutes ago disappeared and was replaced by a somber one. "All kidding aside, that was very brave. I'm glad we both made it through okay, but I'm still having a hard time understanding why the men outside fired. We could easily have taken Carlos."

"Maybe so, but there's nothing that can be done about it now. I think Anthony is right. We're just going to have to find another lead. Have you thought what the next step should be?"

He nodded and pulled his cell phone from his pocket. "I know a guy who may be able to help us."

"Who is he?"

"His name is Rick Thompson. He's a computer genius. We use him a lot to find information for us. Maybe he can help us now." He punched in a number, waited and then frowned. "I got his voice mail." He listened and then left a message. "Rick, this is Seth Dawtry. I need some information on a man named Carlos Allen. He's a former gang member, but we haven't heard much from him over the past few years. See if you can dig up anything on what he might have been doing during that time and give me a call. Thanks."

He finished the call and slipped the phone back in his pocket. "Maybe Rick can come up with something that will help me know which direction to take. Carlos was a gun for hire—if he was attacking Dan, it was on someone's orders. If we can track down who he's been working for, that might give us some answers."

Callie buckled her seat belt and settled back in her seat. "I hope so. Now where are we going?"

"I'm taking you back to my house. I think we need to get Dan's notebook out and look at it again. Maybe he's left a clue somewhere in there that will help us out."

Callie glanced at the clock on the dash. "And I need to check in with the nurses in the Critical Care Unit to see how Uncle Dan is doing. They promised they would call if his condition changed. I haven't heard from them, but I still call them every few hours."

She pulled her cell phone out of her pocket as Seth started the car and pulled into traffic. She'd hoped the nurses would have good news for her, but it wasn't to be tonight. By the time they arrived home, she was beginning to feel the disappointment Seth must have experienced earlier.

Her uncle was barely hanging on to life, and the man who might have answered the question of who wanted him killed was now dead. Ever since she'd gotten off that plane, it had been one horrifying experience after another. When would all this come to an end?

Maybe Uncle Dan's notebook did hold the key to who might have wanted to kill him. If so, it was up to her and Seth to find the answer.

Seth stood at the kitchen sink and stared out over the backyard. He still couldn't believe that Carlos Allen was dead. Just a few hours ago he'd thought he might be on the verge of finding out who was behind all that had happened to Dan and Callie in the past few days. That hope had gone up in smoke when his fellow officers killed Carlos. Now he had to find another way to solve this case.

With a sigh he poured two cups of coffee and set them on the kitchen table. Callie walked in the door at that moment. "Thanks for making coffee. I need some." She slid into one of the chairs and glanced up at him. "I thought your mother would be here, but I didn't see her upstairs."

Seth shook his head. "No, she's off with some of her friends. She left a note saying they were going bowling tonight." He pointed toward the notebook she'd placed on the table. "I've looked at that notebook dozens of times with Dan, and I've never seen anything that led me to any conclusions about Hope. There has to be something that I'm missing."

"Maybe you've always looked for clues about Hope's identity. This time we need to search for anything that might point us in the direction of who wants Uncle Dan dead."

He nodded. "So what do you suggest?"

"I think we should go through this again and look at each page. See if there's anything that he may have added since the last time you looked in here."

"Okay. I can do that."

For the next thirty minutes they turned the pages of the notebook and discussed every detail that Dan had noted on each page, but Seth had seen all this before. Nothing appeared to have been added until Callie turned the page and he saw a flyer for Midtown Mission.

He reached for it. "Where did this come from?"

"You haven't seen this before?"

He shook his head. "I didn't see this the other night when we were looking through the pages, and I don't remember it being here before." The conversation with Melvin popped into his head. "This is the shelter Melvin said he told Dan about, where Carlos does community service. I wonder if Dan got the flyer because of that."

Callie reached for the flyer. "I remember him saying that. Do you know anything about this place?"

"I know it's a well-respected shelter and gives a lot of aid to the homeless. It's run by a woman named Dorothy Tipton. Her picture is in the paper a lot because of all the work she does there."

"Did Uncle Dan volunteer there?"

Seth thought for a moment before he answered. "I never heard him say anything about it."

"Do you think we should go down there and ask Mrs. Tipton about him?"

"I don't know. Let me think about it."

He'd no sooner spoken than his cell phone rang. He pulled it from his pocket, smiled at the caller displayed and pressed the phone to his ear. "Hey, Rick. I can't believe you're already getting back to me about Carlos Allen."

Rick chuckled. "You should have given me somebody more difficult to track down for you. Carlos has been in the mix of things for quite a while now."

Seth reached for the notebook and found a blank page in the back. He pulled a pen from his pocket and waited for what Rick was about to tell him. "Really? Like what?"

Rick took a deep breath. "Well, he's had several arrests over the past few years. Once he was arrested for attempted murder. A gun found at Carlos's house was determined to have been the weapon used, but then it disappeared from the police evidence room. The victim who'd identified him also disappeared. So without a victim or a weapon, the charges against him were dropped."

"Yeah, I remember that now. It happened right after I'd moved to the Cold Case Unit."

"His next arrest came when he was accused of nearly beating a guy to death in a barroom brawl. That time the charges were dropped because the police didn't read him his rights, and the judge threw the case out."

Seth scribbled down the details Rick had just given him. "Anything else?"

"Oh, there's all kinds of little stuff on him over the past ten years or so, but he's never served any time. Most of the time the charges have been reduced, and he's been allowed to do community service work."

"At the Midtown Mission?"

"That's right."

Seth's eyes grew wide, and his heart pounded. "Who approved that?"

"Assistant District Attorney Abby Dalton. It appears she's a big supporter of the mission. I'll send you some links to check out that tell about the mission and its supporters. Her face shows up quite a bit."

"Thanks for all this information, Rick. I appreciate it."

"No problem. I always enjoy working with you guys in the Cold Case Unit. Is there anything else I can help you with?"

Seth thought for a moment. "Yeah, one more thing. Can you find out who arrested Carlos when his rights weren't read to him?"

"I already know the answer to that. It was on the record I saw. Lieutenant Marty Weaver was the arresting officer."

Seth sucked in his breath. "You don't say. That's very interesting. Thanks again, Rick."

"Call if you need anything."

Seth disconnected the call and sat there lost in thought for a moment. "Well," Callie said, "are you going to tell me what he said?"

Seth gave a start and straightened in his chair. "Oh, sorry about that."

For the next few minutes, he replayed the phone conversation for her. When he'd finished, she bit down on her lip and frowned. "So Lieutenant Weaver pops up again. Do you think they might have had some kind of connection?"

Seth pushed to his feet and rubbed the back of his neck. "I don't know. But I'm not about to bring suspicion down on a fellow officer until I have more to go on than I do now."

"I understand that. So what's our next move?"

He chuckled and shook his head. "After what happened tonight, what makes you think there's going to be a next time? When you're not at the hospital with Dan, you need to stay here. That way I can make sure you're safe. A police officer will be out front, and this time you need to take his presence more seriously."

Callie took a deep breath and rose to face him. "I promise I will, but I've been thinking about this. I think the danger to me may be over."

"Oh? What makes you think that?"

"The only way I could be a threat to whoever is after Uncle Dan is by identifying the man who attacked him in the hospital. Carlos had the star tattoo and scar on his face, so I'm sure he's the one I saw in the Critical Care Unit. Now that he's dead, there's no one else I can point to, so maybe we don't need to be so cautious."

Seth smiled. "That's a good try, Callie, but I don't think the threat is going away that easily. You're forgetting the two men at the department store. Even if one of them was Carlos, we still don't know who the other one was. I'm concerned these people will come after you again."

She didn't say anything for a moment. "That may be true, but I still want to get to the bottom of this. Uncle Dan must have had a reason to leave that flyer about the Midtown Mission in his notebook. I know you'll go down there, and I want to be with you. Please don't deny me the chance to help find out who is responsible for everything that's happened."

He started to tell her no, but the pleading look in her eyes made him swallow the words. With a sigh he nodded. "All right. You can go with me to the mission, but you have to do exactly what I say. Understand?"

"Yes, and I promise I won't cause any problems like I did tonight."

"Good. Now I need to get some sleep. I have to be at the office early in the morning, but I can drop you at the hospital on my way and come back for you when I get ready to go to the shelter. You should be safe with the marshal there."

She nodded. "That sounds great. I'll see you at breakfast."

He watched her leave the kitchen before he picked up their coffee cups and carried them to the sink. He stood there a moment, staring out the window into the darkness beyond and thought about what she'd said about not causing him any problems.

The truth was that her very presence caused him a problem. Every time he looked at her he remembered that day two years ago when she'd refused his proposal. All this time he'd tried to tell himself he had dealt with that, but there was still something that puzzled him about her behavior that day. He doubted if he would ever bring full closure to his relationship with Callie until she decided to tell him her real reason.

He groaned and rubbed his hand down his face. What was he doing? It didn't matter what her reason was. Their relationship was history, and he was glad. He'd moved on, and he needed to quit dwelling on the past. Instead, he needed to concentrate on finding out who wanted to kill Dan. That was the most important thing.

And the Midtown Mission just might provide the answers he needed.

SEVEN

The next afternoon, Callie sat beside her uncle's bed in the Critical Care Unit and watched his chest rise and fall in a steady rhythm. She'd been at the hospital since Seth dropped her off early this morning, and she'd kept a silent vigil beside her uncle all day. Although he appeared to be breathing better, he still hadn't regained consciousness. She covered his hand with one of hers and wiped a tear from the corner of her eye with the other.

A nurse stopped outside the door where a deputy U.S. marshal sat and spoke with him a moment before she came into the room. She smiled at Callie, walked around the bed and checked the panel of instruments that displayed vital signs. After a moment she straightened and smiled again. "Everything looks good. He's doing well."

"Then why hasn't he regained consciousness?" Callie asked.

"There's no way of telling when he'll wake up, but don't give up. Keep talking to him like you've been doing. Sometimes patients who've been in comas tell us things that were said to them while they were unconscious."

Callie's eyes grew wide. "Do you think it's possible he can hear me?"

"I don't know, but it's sure worth a try. Let him know you're here."

Callie grasped her uncle's hand tighter and leaned forward until her mouth was closer to his ear. "Uncle Dan, it's Callie. I'm here with you this morning. It's a beautiful day. I wish you would hurry and come back to me so we can get on with our plans. That beach house in Hawaii is still waiting for us, and I would like to take you there. Maybe we can go for you to recover. Would you like to sit on the beach while you're getting your strength back?"

The nurse gave a little chuckle. "Did you see what happened? When you started talking to him about going to Hawaii, his heart rate increased. I think he was giving you an answer. He wants to go as badly as you do."

Tears filled her eyes, and she leaned forward to kiss her uncle's cheek. "We'll be on that plane to Hawaii as soon as you get well. I'm waiting for you."

There was no other movement or change in

his vitals, and in a few minutes Callie stood. The nurse who was in the process of straightening the covers on the bed glanced up. "Are you leaving?"

She shook her head. "No, I think I'll go sit in the waiting room for a while. I'm expecting Detective Dawtry to come for me, and I know he'd like to see Uncle Dan while he's here."

The nurse glanced at her watch. "Family visitation starts in about five minutes. If he gets here in time, he can come in then."

"Thanks. I'll tell him. And I want to thank you for giving me the extra time in here with my uncle today."

She smiled. "It's no problem when everything's quiet in here. Besides, I think he likes having you sit with him."

The marshal sitting outside the cubicle didn't look up from reading a newspaper as Callie walked out, and she didn't stop to chat with him. She headed to the door and exited into the outside hallway before she stepped into the hallway that led to the family waiting room.

As usual, the room was nearly filled today. As she glanced around the area, her gaze came to rest on Seth, who was standing off to the side with a man and woman she'd never seen before. A boy who looked to be about twelve or thirteen years old stood next to Seth. The animated look on his face told her he was enjoying the conversation.

She walked over and stood next to Seth, but he didn't appear to notice her presence for a few moments. "I think that's a great idea, Michael. We need to let the church board know about this right away. We might even be able..." He stopped midsentence when he noticed Callie standing next to him. "Callie," he said, "I didn't hear you come in." He pointed to the couple facing him. "These are my friends Michael and Glenda Bennett and their son, Jeremy, from church."

She smiled at the couple and stuck out her hand. "And I'm Callie Lattimer. Do you have family in the unit?"

Michael shook his head. "Not really family. There's an elderly lady who lives down the street from us. We keep an eye on her because her family lives in Missouri. She fell this morning, and the doctor has put her in the unit for now. We're here to check on her."

"Oh, I see." Callie's gaze drifted over them to the young boy standing next to his father. "And is this your son?"

The boy grinned and ducked his head. Seth reached out and grasped his shoulder. "This is Jeremy. He's going to be the best quarterback Memphis has ever seen when he gets to high school."

Jeremy's face grew red. "Oh, Coach. You tell everybody that. I'm not as good as Freddie Coleman."

Seth's eyes widened. "You're both great players, but you have to remember Freddie is two years older than you. I'm lucky to have both of you on my team."

Callie turned to Seth. "You coach football?"

He nodded. "Yeah. It's the youth league team for our church. I'm not kidding when I say that Jeremy has a real gift for playing football."

Michael reached out and ruffled his son's hair. "Seth has worked untold hours with him, and we really appreciate it."

Glenda nodded. "Seth is great with the kids. We can't figure out why some woman hasn't already snatched him up. He'd make a great husband and a wonderful father. I've tried to fix him up with all my friends, but he's never interested."

Seth's face turned red. "Glenda, I've told you I don't have time for that."

Callie glanced at Jeremy and saw the hero worship for Seth in his eyes, and her heart lurched. Glenda was right. Seth would make a wonderful father. She cleared her throat and turned to Seth. "The nurse said visitation is going to start in a few minutes. You can go in my place this time. They let me sit by his bed for a while this afternoon."

"Are you sure?" he asked.

"It's fine. I think it will do him good to know you're here. I talked to him, and there was some response in his heart rate. See if he reacts to you. While you're with him, I think I'll go get a cup of coffee in the cafeteria. Meet me there when you're finished." She smiled at Glenda and Michael. "It was nice meeting you, and good luck next fall on the football team, Jeremy."

She turned and hurried out of the waiting room before they could say anything more. At the elevator she punched the button and waited for it to stop at her floor. She groaned inwardly and wondered why Glenda's words had upset her. It wasn't as if she and Seth were ever going to get back together, but somehow it had rankled a bit when Glenda spoke of trying to fix him up with her friends.

Callie bit down on her lip and shook her head. She was being ridiculous. Seth was the man she had loved once, but he was only a friend now. She stared down at the floor and rubbed at the tears that threatened to roll down her cheeks.

The elevator door opened, and she stepped inside without looking up. The door closed, and she reached over and pushed the button for the basement level where the cafeteria was located. Behind her someone coughed, and she jerked in surprise. She hadn't noticed anyone at the back of the elevator when she stepped in.

Before she could turn around, a voice she'd heard once before drifted to her ears. "Well, Miss Lattimer. This is a surprise. I didn't expect to run into you today."

Startled, she whirled around and gasped when she saw Lieutenant Marty Weaver standing at the back of the elevator. "Lieutenant Weaver," she said, "I didn't see you."

He smiled and straightened up from leaning against the back wall. "You looked a bit upset when you got in. I hope your uncle isn't worse."

She eased to the far side of the elevator and shook her head. "He's not worse, but he hasn't regained consciousness. I've just been in to see him. What are you doing here?"

"I came to interview a victim of a robbery yesterday. I just got through and was about to go back to the station. Are you leaving?"

His eyes narrowed, and his gaze swept her. Something about the way he looked at her made her skin prickle. "N-no. I'm going to the cafeteria for a cup of coffee. Seth is going to meet me there in a few minutes."

He glanced at his watch and smiled. "A cup of

coffee sounds good, and I have a little time before I need to report back in. Mind if I join you?"

Callie searched her mind for a reason for wanting to be alone, but she could think of nothing. "I guess not."

The elevator came to a stop on the ground floor. He smiled and gestured as the door opened. "After you, Miss Lattimer."

Callie straightened her shoulders and headed into the cafeteria toward the coffee machine, but Lieutenant Weaver's voice behind her stopped her. "I'll get our coffee. You find us a table."

With a nod she glanced around the cafeteria and spotted a table in the center of the room. She'd just slid into her chair when he ambled up to the table with two cups in his hands. He set them down, placed his hat on the table and dropped into a chair. She took a sip from her cup and stared at him over the rim.

He was younger than she had first thought yesterday, probably mid-thirties. His dark, curly hair had some streaks of gray around the edges, but it added a distinguished look. But it was his eyes that made chills run down her spine. She had always believed the old saying that eyes were the windows to the soul, but when she looked into Marty Weaver's, they appeared completely blank.

"Thank you for the coffee," she murmured.

He took a swig from his cup, set it down and crossed his arms on the table. "You're welcome. So tell me about yourself, Callie." He hesitated a moment. "May I call you Callie? I've heard your uncle talk about you so much I feel I already know you."

She frowned and took another drink. "I didn't realize you knew my uncle that well."

He nodded. "Oh, yeah. I've known Judge Lattimer for quite a while. I volunteer at the youth center where he does."

"I didn't realize that."

"Yeah. He told me you're a college professor."

"I am. I teach at the University of Virginia."

"Too bad about what happened to him. He'd said the two of you were going to Hawaii for his retirement."

Lieutenant Weaver's words were friendly enough, but they lacked any kind of emotion. Added to her growing unease was the picture of this man standing over Carlos Allen's lifeless body. As she remembered it, Marty Weaver hadn't appeared to be concerned at all.

Her hands began to shake. She clenched her fists and stuck them in her lap. What was keeping Seth? She took a deep breath and tried to smile.

"It was nice of you to keep me company, Lieutenant Weaver…"

"Marty," he interrupted. "Please call me Marty."

"All right, Marty. As I was saying, it was nice of you to keep me company, but I really don't want to detain you. If you need to get back to headquarters, I understand."

He shook his head and took another drink of his coffee. "I'm in no hurry. To tell you the truth, I was glad to see you when you stepped in that elevator. I've been thinking about you since I saw you yesterday outside that bar. You looked very upset."

"I *was* upset. It's not every day I see a man killed. Especially someone I had hoped would have information about the attempts on my uncle's life."

He nodded. "I can understand that." He leaned closer. "I know you're having a tough time right now with your uncle hurt, but I want to let you know I'd be happy to help you any way I can."

The words surprised Callie, and she blinked. "Help me?"

"You know, like try to take your mind off things for a while. Maybe you'd have dinner with me one night."

Callie swallowed hard and stared at him. "You want to take me to dinner?"

"Yeah. How about it?"

A shadow fell across the table, and Callie

glanced up to see Seth towering over them. "How about what?" he asked.

Marty shrugged. "Nothing to concern yourself with, Dawtry. This was a private conversation between Callie and me."

Seth darted a glance at Callie. "Really? Am I interrupting?"

Callie shook her head. "No, Marty and I were just having a cup of coffee together. How was your visit with Uncle Dan?"

"No change. He didn't respond at all to me."

Callie sighed, stood up, then looked back at Marty. "I have to go now. Seth and I have something we have to do. Maybe we'll meet again."

He stood up and glanced from her to Seth. "Maybe we will. Think about what I said, though. I really meant it."

She bit down on her lip and nodded. Marty picked up his hat and placed it on his head before he strode toward the door. Seth didn't speak until he was out of sight.

"What was he asking you when I walked up?"

Callie scooted her chair up under the table and shrugged. "Nothing, really. He said he'd like to take me to dinner."

"He what?" Seth's words exploded from his mouth, and two people at a table across the room looked up in surprise.

"Seth," Callie whispered, "keep your voice

down. I said he asked. I didn't accept. I couldn't go out with him. There's something about him that scares me."

The muscle in Seth's jaw flexed, and his nostrils flared. After a moment he took a deep breath. "I'm sorry, Callie. It's none of my business who you go out with. I'm sure you can make your own decisions without any help from me. Now let's go. I'd like to get down to the homeless shelter before they open the doors for the night."

Callie's mouth dropped open, and she stared in disbelief as Seth turned and strode from the room. Did he really think she could have any interest in Marty Weaver? The way he was acting she might think he was jealous if she didn't know better.

Ever since she'd been back, he'd been quick to let her know that his feelings for her had died two years ago. Maybe he didn't want her anymore, but he didn't want anyone else to have her, either. That seemed like such a childish attitude to her.

Then she remembered Glenda's comment earlier that Seth would make a great husband and father and how she'd reacted to it. Neither she nor Seth had moved on since their breakup, and maybe it was time she did something to give them a shove to do so.

She needed something to help her begin to move forward, but it wasn't going to be a date with Marty Weaver.

Seth tried to concentrate on the traffic as he drove, but his thoughts kept returning to what had happened in the hospital cafeteria. He couldn't believe how irrationally he'd acted. What did it matter to him who Callie dated? But Marty Weaver? He'd never liked the man, even though he knew Dan had been friends with him through the youth center. Dan, who always looked for the best in everyone, had often told him he needed to be more accepting of people he didn't understand, that it was difficult to know a person until you'd walked in their shoes.

He wondered how Dan would feel knowing that Weaver had seemed unconcerned with the death of a man they'd needed to take into custody yesterday. Seth still hadn't accepted the fact that the officers outside had shot first instead of trying to disarm him. But then he hadn't been able to do it inside the bar, so maybe he didn't need to judge those outside so quickly. That was one thing Dan had always cautioned him about—don't come to a conclusion until you have all the facts.

His throat closed, and he felt tears sting his eyes. He couldn't stand to think of Dan in that hospital bed, so still and unresponsive. For years he'd been a role model for Seth, and he didn't know how he could go on without him. And if Dan died, what would happen to Callie?

She'd made it clear two years ago that their future wasn't together, but he still cared what happened to her. He wanted her to find someone who'd make her happy. Even if he didn't like Marty Weaver, it wasn't up to him to make choices for her about her life.

He took a deep breath. "I'm sorry for the way I reacted back there in the cafeteria. You have the right to date anyone you choose. If you want to go out with Marty, I'm okay with that."

She turned a cool gaze on him, and he almost shivered at the frosty look in her eyes. "I must say that makes me feel a lot better, Detective Dawtry, to know that all my dates don't have to apply to you for approval."

His mouth dropped open, and his eyes grew wide. "What is that supposed to mean? I was trying to be nice."

"Well, don't do me any favors," she snapped. "I will go out with whoever I want and whenever I want. And when I decide to do so, I won't be asking your permission."

Before he could voice a reply, she turned her head and stared out the car window. He exhaled deeply and directed his attention back to the afternoon traffic. Neither of them spoke as he drove toward the shelter.

When he pulled into the parking lot at the Midtown Mission, he wasn't surprised to see several homeless people standing on the sidewalk in front of the building. Since there weren't enough beds to supply the ones needing them, many had started showing up early in hopes of being lucky enough to get a place before they were all gone.

Seth pulled to a stop and turned the engine off. He curled his fingers around the steering wheel and tightened them before he turned to look toward Callie. She had her hands folded in her lap and stared down at them.

He swallowed and took a deep breath. "Callie, I'm sorry for the way I acted. Please forgive me if I made you feel uncomfortable in any way. All I want is for you to be happy."

She glanced up, and tears sparkled in her eyes. "That's all I want for you, too, Seth, but I'm afraid our being together so much isn't working out very well. Maybe it would be better if I went to a hotel."

He shook his head. "No, you can't do that. We're not sure the threat to your life is over, and I need to keep you close so I can protect you in case anyone comes after you again."

"But Seth…"

He held up a hand to stop her. "No. We're going to make this situation work. Last night we were determined to be friends for Dan's sake so we could all enjoy spending time together when he recovers. Today we seem to have forgotten that." He reached over and touched her arm. "I'm really trying to let go of what happened between us, but I have to admit it's hard. I still don't understand why you left, and I may never, but I'm sincere when I say I want to be your friend."

She stared down at his hand before she covered it with hers and smiled. "I want to be your friend, too, Seth. I'm sorry for the way I spoke to you, but you need to understand that you can't decide who I will go out with."

"I understand that."

"And I want you to feel free to date anyone you choose. So let's not argue over things that we can't control for each other. From now on let's concentrate on finding out who Hope is and why someone is trying to kill Uncle Dan. If we can do that, then I'll leave Memphis as soon as he's well enough to travel, and you won't be troubled with me anymore."

He started to protest that she didn't trouble him, but he decided against it. Instead, he nodded. "Let's go see what we can find out inside."

They got out of the car and walked toward

the mission. As they approached the front door, several homeless men who'd been standing in front of the door moved out of their way and stared at them as they walked past. There was a stir among the people on the sidewalk as the smell of bread baking drifted outside. Seth held the door open for Callie and followed her inside.

It had been several months since Seth had been inside the building, but it looked no different now than it had then. The room they entered served as the dining room, and rows of tables lined the floor. Folding chairs had been placed at each spot, which would later in the evening provide a seat for a hungry person to enjoy a free meal.

The banging of pots and pans echoed from the room at the back, and he headed to the door that led into that area of the building. He stopped just inside the kitchen with Callie behind him and let his gaze drift over the room. Steam rose from several large pots on a stove where a woman wearing a long, white apron appeared to be overseeing their progress. Another woman chopped vegetables at a table, and a third looked up from smoothing the icing on top of a cake.

"Hello, may I help you?"

Seth nodded. "I'd like to see Dorothy Tipton if she's available."

The woman wiped her hands on her apron

and walked over to them. "Mrs. Tipton is in her office down the hall. Who should I tell her wants to speak with her?"

Seth pulled out his badge. "Detective Seth Dawtry with the Memphis Police."

She nodded and stepped around them. "Follow me."

They followed her down a narrow hallway that led from the dining room toward the back of the building and stopped outside a closed door. She knocked on the door. "Mrs. Tipton?"

"Yes." The muffled voice could barely be heard through the closed door.

"There's someone here to see you."

A moment later the door opened, and a woman who looked to be in her late fifties stood before them. "Who is it?"

"He's a police officer, Mrs. Tipton. He needs to speak with you."

She glanced past the woman to Seth. "Of course. Won't you come in?"

The woman from the kitchen stepped out of the way, and Callie and Seth walked into the room. Mrs. Tipton pointed to two chairs facing the desk. "Please have a seat."

"Thank you," Seth said as he and Callie took their seats.

Mrs. Tipton waited until they were settled before she walked behind her desk and sat in the chair there. She folded her hands and leaned forward. "Now how may I help you?"

Seth straightened in his chair. "I'm Detective Seth Dawtry with the Memphis PD, and this is my friend Dr. Callie Lattimer. Her uncle is Judge Dan Lattimer. You may know him."

A sad look creased her face, and she looked at Callie. "I do. I was so sorry to hear he's been in an accident. How is he doing?"

"He's holding his own. We're very hopeful he's going to be all right."

"I'm glad to hear that."

"We're here, Mrs. Tipton," Seth said, "because we thought you might be able to help us with something. The police have reason to believe that one of the people who might have been responsible for Judge Lattimer's wreck was Carlos Allen, who seems to have a long history with this mission. I wondered if you could tell us anything about him."

She chewed on her lip and nodded. "I know Carlos. This mission also serves as a type of halfway house where individuals can do court-ordered community service hours. Through the years Carlos has served a lot of time here. I've always liked him, and I believe he could really make something of his life. But he's never been able to break away from that criminal mentality he's had for years. I haven't seen him in a while, so I hoped he was finally doing better."

"I'm afraid you won't be seeing him at all anymore. He was shot to death by police last night."

Mrs. Tipton's eyes widened, and she gasped. "Oh, no. I'm sorry to hear that."

"I was, too," Seth said. "But you said he'd been here a lot over the years. Do you know why he kept getting assigned here instead of spending time in jail?"

She shook her head. "I'm afraid I can't answer that. I only follow the court's recommendations and take the offenders they send. If you'd like more information, I suggest you talk with Assistant District Attorney Abby Dalton. She's one of our greatest supporters, and she keeps an eye out for offenders she thinks might benefit from doing community service hours instead of spending time behind bars."

Seth nodded and pushed to his feet. "I'll do that. Thank you for your time, Mrs. Tipton. I appreciate the help you've been."

She rose and walked around her desk to the door. "If you think of anything else you'd like to ask me, come again. I'm here every day, even Sundays. We have a morning worship service before lunch." She opened the door and stuck out her hand to Callie. "I am praying for your uncle's recovery, Dr. Lattimer. Please let him know."

Callie shook her hand and smiled. "Thank you, and please call me Callie. I was wondering, though, what kind of qualifications you need to volunteer here?"

Mrs. Tipton glanced from Callie to Seth. "Are you thinking of volunteering? We already have a doctor and nurse who provide us with health needs."

Callie chuckled. "I'm not that kind of doctor, Mrs. Tipton. I'm a PhD who is willing to roll up her sleeves and help when she sees a need. I know my uncle supported this place, and I would like to do it in his honor."

Mrs. Tipton smiled and squeezed her hand. "Whenever you want to come here, give me a call. I can always use an extra pair of hands."

"Thank you. I'll let you know."

Seth couldn't believe the exchange he'd just heard, and he followed Callie from the building without saying a word. He didn't speak until they were back in the car. Then he swiveled in his seat and faced her. "What was that all about?"

She turned to face him and blinked. "What are you talking about?"

"Why would you ask about volunteering?"

"I may not be a trained police officer, Seth,

but I can tell when something doesn't make sense. Why would a repeat offender like Carlos Allen keep getting community service instead of going to jail? There's something wrong in the system somewhere. It's either in the courts, here at the center or they're working together. It might help to have somebody undercover to find out where the problem is."

He shook his head. "I can guarantee it's not going to be you undercover."

She smiled and reached for her seat belt. "We can deal with that situation when we decide where the problem may lie. For now, why don't we go to see A.D.A. Dalton?"

Seth started to restate his opposition to her proposal, but he groaned and pulled his seat belt tight as he decided to pick his battles. He really didn't know if he was more upset at the prospect of her going undercover at the mission or the fact that she had thought of doing it before he had.

Having a pair of eyes inside the shelter might help the investigation. "It's not a bad idea, Callie. But like you said, let's talk to Ms. Dalton and find out how Carlos Allen got away with doing so much community service time instead of being behind bars. She should have some 7interesting answers for us."

EIGHT

Seth had barely said anything to her ever since they'd left the mission, and Callie was beginning to wonder if he was truly upset over her suggestion. She studied his profile out of the corner of her eye as they entered the building that housed the District Attorney's offices and took the elevator to the third floor.

When they stepped off the elevator, Callie could hold her tongue no longer. She stopped in the hallway and put her hand on Seth's arm. "Is something wrong? You've been way too quiet."

He shook his head. "What you said back there about volunteering has gotten me thinking. I shouldn't bring you into this investigation. It's dangerous, and you're not used to dealing with situations like this. I can't run the risk of your getting hurt. How could I explain that to Dan?"

She sighed and shook her head. "Seth, we're never going to find out anything if you keep trying to protect me. I feel like we're on the verge of discovering something that may lead to some answers, and we have to go forward. I'm willing for you to take the lead, but I want to be there with you."

He looked at her, then pointed down the hallway. "Behind the doors down this hallway are the assistant D.A.s I work with all the time. I have never brought a person who has a special interest in a crime to a meeting before. I don't think Ms. Dalton will want you in there when I see her."

"I can understand that. Why don't I wait outside in the hall? I see a bench against the wall down there, and I can sit there while you're inside with her."

"You'd be willing to do that?"

She laughed. "Of course I would. I want to do whatever it takes to find out some answers."

"Then that's settled. Let's go."

At that moment another elevator door opened, and a woman who appeared to be her mid-thirties stepped off. She wore a black skirt with a matching jacket, and her blond hair was pulled into a bun at the back of her head. Small-framed glasses perched on the end of her nose. She smiled when she saw Seth. "Detective Dawtry, how are you today?"

"I'm good. In fact, I'm here to see you." Her gaze swept Callie, and he nodded in her direction. "Abby Dalton, this is Judge Lattimer's niece, Callie."

Her eyes darkened, and she stuck her hand out. "I was so sorry to hear about your uncle. How is he?"

Callie grasped her hand and shook it. "He's holding his own."

"Good." She turned back to Seth. "You wanted to see me?"

"Yes. Could we talk in your office?"

"Sure." She darted a glance at Callie.

Callie pointed to the bench she'd mentioned earlier. "You two go on. I'll wait here for you, Seth. It was nice to meet you, Ms. Dalton."

"And you, Callie. I'm praying for your uncle's recovery."

"Thank you."

Callie sank down on the bench as Seth and Abby disappeared into her office. How she wished she could be a fly on the wall and hear what they would say, but she knew she had done the right thing. Seth needed to follow police regulations, and having a victim of a crime present while he was talking with the District Attorney's office might have raised some red flags. Still, she wished she could have been in there. She sighed and settled back on the bench.

A door down the hall opened, and a man who looked familiar stepped out into the hallway and walked toward her. He stopped when he drew even with the bench. "Excuse me. Aren't you Callie Lattimer?"

She looked up into the dark eyes of the man she knew she'd seen somewhere before, but she couldn't quite place him. "Yes. I'm sorry. Have we met?"

He smiled and nodded. "My name is Brad Austin. I'm one of Seth's partners. You came with Judge Lattimer to my wedding."

The memory of a night two years before popped into her head, and she smiled. "Of course, Brad. I'm sorry I didn't recognize you. I enjoyed that night so much." She scooted over and pointed to the bench. "Would you like to sit down?"

He looked at his watch, then nodded and settled onto the bench. "What are you doing sitting out here all alone?"

"I'm waiting for Seth. He's in talking with Abby Dalton right now."

Brad nodded. "I couldn't believe it when I saw you out here alone. I've been to the hospital several times to check on your uncle, but it's been when you weren't there. How is he today?"

She shook her head. "He's about the same. I just wish he would regain consciousness."

He glanced toward Abby's door. "I've talked to Seth several times. He's really been torn up about what happened to your uncle. You know he loves him like a father."

Callie's throat tightened, and she swallowed. "I know."

"Seth and Alex, our other partner, are two of the best friends a guy could ever have. He's talked to me a lot about how much he missed having a father who loved him when he was growing up. Your uncle has made a real difference in his life. More than being a father figure, he's also the one who led Seth to his faith in God. That has gotten him through a lot of tough spots in his life."

"I'm glad to know that."

"Seth says that Dan talks a lot about how worried he was when you came to live with him that he couldn't be a good father. He has tried to pass on to Seth what he learned." Brad smiled. "But I'd have to say Dan did a good job. Look at how successful you are. Dan is really proud of what you've accomplished."

Tears gathered in the corners of her eyes. "Thank you for telling me that. I owe him a lot—and I love him very much."

Brad took a deep breath. "I need to get back to the office. Tell Seth I'll see him there later." He started to rise but hesitated. "But better than that, tell him Laura and I would really like for him to bring you to dinner at our house. Laura's a nurse at the hospital, and she's been checking on your uncle, too. She'd mentioned having you over. That'll give us a chance to get to know each other better."

"I'd like that, Brad. Thanks for the invitation."

His smile deepened. "And it'll also give us a chance to show off our son. He's the center of our world, and he loves Seth."

"He does?"

Brad chuckled. "You ought to see Seth with him. If ever a guy was cut out to be a father, he was." He pushed to his feet. "I've got to get out of here. It was good to see you, Callie, and don't forget about the invitation. I'll remind Seth, too."

She nodded. "I'll tell him, and tell your wife thank-you for checking on my uncle. Maybe we'll see you soon."

Callie managed to hold on to her smile until the elevator door closed behind Brad. Then she slumped against the back of the bench and let the tears stream down her cheeks.

Two men in different places had said the same thing to her today. Seth would make a wonderful father.

She clenched her fists and pounded her knees. Why did she have to keep being reminded of something that she knew to be true? Seth *would* make a wonderful father, and she'd given him the chance to do that when she'd refused his marriage proposal.

The thing that bothered her, though, was that he didn't seem to be moving on like she'd thought he would. Several times he'd hinted that he still didn't understand why she had said no. Maybe it would be better if she told him the real reason, but she wasn't sure how he would react to the truth.

She sighed and wiped the tears from her eyes. Better to leave things as they were. In time he would find a woman he could love. Then he'd be able to have the family he deserved. Even if it still hurt at times to think about him married to someone else, she had to admit it was better than having him come to hate her because he was saddled with a wife who could never give him children.

Seth sat in the chair facing Abby Dalton's desk and thought of Callie waiting in the hall for him. He'd been surprised when she'd volunteered to wait outside, but she'd been right. Abby might not have opened up if someone who wasn't involved in law enforcement had been present.

He settled in his seat, propped his elbows on the chair arms and clasped his hands in front of him. "Thanks for seeing me."

"No problem. Is there something I can help you with about one of your cold cases?"

"It involves one of my cold cases that may be linked to an investigation right now. I'm looking into how Judge Lattimer's attack may be related to a cold case that happened twenty-five years ago."

"Twenty-five years ago? I was only a child then, so I don't know that I'll have any information for you about a case that old." She frowned. "Why would the attempts on Judge Lattimer's life have anything to do with something that happened so long ago?"

For the next few minutes Seth explained the case involving the murder victim Dan had called Hope and how he believed the attacks in the car and at the hospital were attempts at silencing him. He told her about a street informant who had identified Carlos Allen as the hit man and how Carlos had been killed at Sam's Bar and Grill.

When he finished, she pulled off her glasses and laid them on her desk. "I heard about the shooting of Carlos. I hated that. I'd hoped he was getting away from the criminal lifestyle after his last run-in with the law."

"That's something I don't understand," Seth said. "Carlos has a long rap sheet. He seemed to be in court time after time, but he never went to jail. He was always given community service hours. Do you know why?"

She shrugged. "It's simple, Detective. Our jails are crowded, and the courts are hesitant to keep sending offenders there unless we can prove beyond a reasonable doubt that they're a threat to society."

Seth's eyebrows arched. "And you thought Carlos wasn't a threat? The man died in a shoot-out with police. He pulled a gun on me in a bar and was about to start shooting without any thought of innocent bystanders. I'd say he was a grave threat to society."

"It doesn't matter what you or I would say—all that matters is what can be proven at trial. I know at times the police don't agree with what this office does. My only response is if the arresting officers would be more careful about what they do then we here at the prosecutor's office might have an easier time when we went into court."

Seth frowned. "What's that supposed to mean?"

"It means that several times when I got ready to prosecute Carlos it was suddenly discovered that the evidence against him had disappeared from the evidence room. There's no way I can get a conviction just because an officer believes something to be true. I have to have hard evidence. Once he was denied a lawyer after he'd asked for one, and the last time Carlos was arrested, the case was thrown out because nobody read him his rights. Those kinds of cases can't be won, Detective."

"So you're saying the police are at fault in a lot of these instances?"

"That's exactly what I'm saying. With the weak evidence that I had, there was no way I could win those cases, so I took plea bargains that kept them from being complete acquittals. I thought I was doing a service to Carlos and to society by getting him to agree to do community service, and the judge authorized it."

Seth pondered what she'd said for a moment before he spoke. "Do you assign all of your offenders who do community service to the Midtown Mission?"

"No. Why?"

"I noticed that all of Carlos's time was spent there."

"Really? I wasn't aware of that, but it doesn't surprise me. The Midtown Mission is one of my pet charities. They do a great job, and I feel confident they'll work with the people I send to them." She glanced at her watch. "Is there anything else? I have a meeting with the District Attorney in his office in ten minutes, and I need to get my notes together."

He stood and stuck out his hand. "Then I don't

want to take up any more of your time. Thank you for seeing me today. I'll see myself out."

She smiled and shook his hand. "I hope I was of help. Come back anytime. My door is always open to the police."

At the door he glanced over his shoulder, but she was already looking at a piece of paper she'd pulled from a folder. He exited the office and stepped into the hall where Callie waited. She rose from the bench when he stepped into the hallway and smiled, but her lips trembled a bit.

He frowned and stepped closer. "What's wrong? You look pale."

She laughed and shook her head. "I'm okay. I was thinking about Uncle Dan." She inhaled and swallowed. "How did your meeting go?"

He glanced around as a door down the hall opened, and two women stepped out. "I'll tell you when we get in the car," he whispered.

They walked to the elevator, and as they waited the two women ambled up behind them and stopped. "I'm glad you suggested a break," one of them said. "I've been working on those files all day, and I still haven't finished."

"Donna, you don't have to do it all today. You've got until next week."

"I know, but I have some other things I need to

work on before the D.A. gets back from his trip. I promised him the files would be my priority."

Seth's body stiffened at the words he'd just heard. He turned, faced the women and smiled. "Excuse me, but I couldn't help but overhear. I'm Detective Seth Dawtry with the Memphis PD, and I was hoping to get an appointment with the D.A. I just heard you say he's out of town. When will he be back?"

The one he supposed to be Donna smiled. "He's gone to a meeting in New Orleans and should be back a week from today. I take care of his calendar. I'll be glad to set it up for you."

"Thanks. I'll call when I see what my schedule is like."

The elevator arrived at that moment, and the four of them stepped inside. When the doors opened on the ground floor, Seth allowed the two women to walk out before he and Callie headed toward the front door.

Once on the sidewalk, Callie glanced up at him. "What do you need to see the D.A. about?"

"Several things," he said. "One being why an assistant D.A. just told me she had a meeting with him in his office in ten minutes. The lady who takes care of his calendar said he wouldn't be back for a week."

Callie's eyes widened. "Abby Dalton lied to you?"

"Yes."

"Why would she do that?"

"I don't know, but I'm going to find out."

NINE

On Saturday afternoon Callie hummed a familiar tune as she folded her laundry and put it away. She picked up a pair of capris and frowned when she remembered these were the pants she was getting ready to buy when she'd been abducted. She shook her head and tried to think of something more pleasant.

Her uncle still hadn't regained consciousness, but his vital signs improved every day. The doctors were now sure it was just a matter of time until he opened his eyes. She looked forward to that happening, but in some ways she dreaded it. That's when the hard work would begin with the rehab he would need to restart his life.

"Callie, can you come downstairs?" Seth's voice echoed up the stairway.

She opened the bedroom door and called back. "Be there in a minute."

Over the past few days, Seth had been busy at work, and she had hardly seen him except for him to drive her to the hospital in the mornings and pick her up later for the return trip home. She'd spent most of her afternoons on the new computer she'd bought after the fire. Fall would be here before she knew it, and she had to get the syllabus ready for each of her classes.

Somehow working on the lesson plans and assignments for her classes hadn't given her as much pleasure as it usually did. The uncertainty over Uncle Dan's condition loomed in the back of her mind. She hoped he would be well enough to be transferred to Virginia before fall classes began.

She hung the capris in her closet then headed downstairs. Seth sat at the kitchen table with a cup of coffee in front of him. He looked up and smiled when she walked in. "Would you like some coffee?"

"I would, but I'll get it."

He didn't say anything else until she was seated at the table with her cup. Then he smiled. "Mom just left to meet some of her friends for their Saturday afternoon movie outing. They're going out to dinner afterward, so she won't be home until later."

Callie nodded. "She told me while we were shopping she had plans. I'm so glad she stays busy. Uncle Dan always has, too. I hope he gets the chance to do it again."

"He will. Just give it some time." He picked up a spoon and stirred his coffee. "It looks like we're on our own for dinner."

Callie shook her head. "That's all right. I feel like I've monopolized your time since I've been here, and you haven't gotten to do anything with your friends. If you want to go out tonight, don't worry about me. I have a lot of work to do, and I can find something to eat. Your mother keeps a well-stocked refrigerator."

He tilted his head to one side and stared down into his cup. "There is something I'd like to do with my friends tonight, but they've asked you to come along, too."

Her eyebrows arched. "Really? What is it?"

"Brad called. He and Laura are having a few friends in for a cookout, and he's asked us to come."

"That's so nice of him. He told me the other day he'd like for us to get together, but I thought he was just being polite."

"Where did you see him?"

"He stopped and talked to me when I was waiting for you outside Abby Dalton's office. He said his wife has been checking on my uncle."

Seth nodded. "Laura works at the hospital counseling families who have experienced violent crimes. They have a little boy who's the cutest kid I've ever seen. Alex and Grace Crowne are going to be there, too."

Callie's brow wrinkled. "So these are your partners in the Cold Case Unit?"

"Yeah, and the two best friends I've ever had. They're great guys, and I think you'd really like their wives. Alex's wife, Grace, is the anchor on the news for WKIZ-TV."

"Oh, I've seen her on TV several times since I've been here, but I didn't realize that she was your partner's wife."

He put his spoon down and leaned closer. "So how about it? Would you go to a cookout with my friends?"

She'd promised herself she wouldn't involve herself in Seth's life any more than she already had. So the smart thing to do would be to say no.

She opened her mouth to say so, but the hopeful look on his face pierced her heart. He had done everything he could to help her and her uncle since she'd arrived in Memphis. The least she could do was go to a cookout with his friends. After all, it was only this once. She probably would never see any of them again.

She smiled. "All right. I'll go."

He exhaled and grinned. "Good. I'll call Brad and tell him we'll be there. They said come about seven. Is that okay with you?"

"Seven is fine." She pushed back from the

table and rose. "I think I'll go upstairs and pick out an outfit. Then I need to do some work on my fall classes. What time do we need to leave?"

"It takes about thirty minutes to drive to Brad and Laura's. Six-thirty okay with you?"

"It is. I'll see you then."

Callie turned and headed out of the kitchen. As she climbed the stairs to her bedroom, she shook her head in despair. If she had accepted Seth's proposal two years ago, she might very well be friends with both Laura and Grace. But she hadn't, and now she was going to spend the evening with them with the stigma of being the woman who'd broke Seth's heart hanging over her.

She shouldn't have accepted this invitation. The last thing she needed was to be around two couples who she imagined were very much in love and who blamed her for Seth not getting on with his life. Then there was Brad and Laura's child. Seth said he was the cutest kid he'd ever seen, and Brad had said the little boy adored Seth.

At the top of the stairs, she stopped on the landing and took a deep breath. She'd faced challenges before, and she would again. But she feared tonight might be the worst one she'd ever had to endure.

* * *

Seth glanced at his watch as he and Callie got out of the car at Brad and Laura's house. He didn't know why he was so nervous. It wasn't like he was bringing a date to meet his friends. They knew Dan, and they had met Callie at Brad and Laura's wedding. Still, they knew he'd been through a rough patch because of her, and he hoped they could put that aside for the night.

He rang the doorbell, and the door swung open. Grace Crowne smiled at them from behind the storm door and pushed it open for them to enter. "Seth, come on in."

They stepped into the entry, and Seth turned to Callie. "Grace, this is Callie Lattimer. I don't know if you've met her before."

Grace's eyes sparkled, and a big smile flashed on her face. She grabbed Callie's hand. "I remember seeing you at Brad and Laura's wedding, but to tell you the truth, that night is almost a blur to me. Alex and I were feuding at the time, and we happened to be the ones standing up with the bride and groom. It wasn't a good night for me."

Callie shook her hand and smiled. "I remember seeing you there, and I've watched you on TV several times since I've been back home.

You are so relaxed behind the camera. I don't know how you do it."

Grace looped her arm through Callie's and guided her down the hallway. "We're all blessed in different ways. Now me, I could never be a teacher, and I'll bet you love it."

"I do."

Grace glanced over her shoulder at Seth, who followed behind them. "Why don't you go on out to the patio? The guys are out there, and Brad has a cooler of soft drinks. You and Alex can keep him company while he cooks the hamburgers."

Seth nodded. "That sounds great."

"I'll take care of Callie," Grace said as she led her into the kitchen.

From inside he heard Laura welcome Callie, and he smiled. Maybe he'd been worried about nothing. Everything appeared to be going fine. He walked to the door at the end of the hallway and stepped outside. Alex Crowne and Brad Austin lounged in chairs at the table in the middle of the patio. Smoke curled up from a grill a few feet away.

Seth laughed when he saw the two. "I knew I should have gotten here earlier. You guys always let the burgers burn if I'm not here to keep an eye on you."

"Yeah, sure," Alex scoffed. "I remember

that last cookout at your house. Thank goodness your mother was there that night. We almost had to go for takeout before she rescued the hot dogs."

Seth grinned, reached in the cooler and pulled out a canned soft drink. He flipped the tab, sank down in a chair and took a drink. "Mmm, that's good."

Brad pushed to his feet and walked to the grill. "So how's Dan today?"

"About the same. Vital signs are stronger, but he's still unconscious. Callie told me she saw you the other day."

Brad nodded. "Yeah, outside Abby Dalton's office. What were you doing there?"

For the next few minutes he told them about Carlos Allen's community service hours and how he hadn't served time in jail. "It seems to me that a judge would start to notice that an offender was getting off a lot with community service."

"Not if the cases are handled by different judges," Alex said.

Seth shrugged. "That's true. Things just don't add up with Carlos Allen, though. I still wonder why the officers outside the bar didn't try to take Carlos alive. Marty Weaver didn't like me questioning their actions, though."

Alex snapped his fingers, and his eyebrows

arched. "Hey, guys, that reminds me. I forgot to ask you something yesterday at work."

Brad came over to the table and sat down. "What?"

"Why would Marty Weaver have any interest in that racketeering case we're looking into?"

Seth and Brad glanced at each other and frowned. "You mean the five-year-old unsolved murder of the laundry owner who was killed after complaining to the police that an extortion ring was demanding protection money from him every month?" Brad asked.

Alex nodded. "That's the one. I went down to the evidence room yesterday to see if there was anything we'd overlooked. When I started to sign in, I saw Marty's name on there from that morning. I asked the officer if anyone else had been looking at the evidence in our case, and he said Marty had been the last one."

Seth leaned forward. "Marty Weaver came to the evidence room and looked at our crime scene evidence?"

"Yes. Why would he do that?"

Seth shook his head. "I don't know. Who investigated that murder when it happened?"

"Maybe we need to find out," Brad said.

Seth curled his fingers around his soft drink can and thought for a moment. "There should still be an active investigation into the racketeering ring that extorts money from small-business owners. Have either of you heard anything lately?"

"No," Brad said, "but we need to look into that. I'll get started on it Monday morning."

"Excuse me, guys." Laura's voice startled the three of them, and they glanced up to see her standing at the table with Callie behind her. Both held bowls of food. "I thought we had a rule we didn't talk about work on nights when we were together." She glanced at the grill. "I hope you haven't let the burgers burn while you were discussing your case."

Brad jumped to his feet and kissed his wife on the cheek. "They're coming right up, ma'am."

Her gaze followed him as he rushed back to the grill and began to pile the hamburgers onto a platter. The back door opened, and Grace stepped out. She held Brad and Laura's son, Mark, in her arms, and she beamed as she walked across the backyard.

"This young man is ready to join the party if someone will be kind enough to bring his high chair outside," she said.

Alex pushed up from his chair. "I'll do it if the rest of you can get the food ready."

Seth rose and came around the table to where Grace stood. The baby smiled when he saw him and held out his arms for Seth to take him. He laughed and took the child from Grace. He glanced over at Callie. "This is my best buddy. His name is Mark. He's named after Laura's brother."

Callie's gaze drifted over him and Mark before she blinked and looked back at him. She smiled, but her eyes held a sad look. "I met Mark while I was inside. I understand why you said he was the cutest kid you've ever seen."

Seth had seen that look in her eyes once before, the night she'd refused his proposal. He didn't understand it then, and he didn't now. How he wished he could penetrate the veil that shielded her innermost thoughts and feelings from him. Before he could ask her what was wrong, Alex came out the back door with the high chair.

"Here we are," he said.

He set the chair down next to the table, and Seth glanced at Callie once more. She had turned her attention toward Brad. Seth pulled Mark close, kissed the top of his head and slipped the child into the chair. He slid the tray into position and stepped back.

"Hold on there, Seth," Alex said. "We need to put the seat belt around his waist. We want to make sure he's secure."

Laura laughed and punched Grace in the

arm. "Listen to your husband. He sounds like a child expert."

Grace smiled, walked over to Alex and slid her arm around his waist. He looked down at her and pulled her next to him. They stood side by side, smiling at their friends. "If he isn't a child expert," Grace said, "he'd better start practicing because we found out this week we're going to have a baby."

"What?" Laura squealed before she ran to Grace and wrapped her in a hug. Then she put her hands on Grace's shoulders and held her at arm's length. "Why didn't you tell me?"

Grace laughed. "We told our parents first, and we wanted to tell you when we were all together."

Laura turned to her husband. "Brad, isn't this great?"

Brad grabbed Alex's hand and pumped it. "It sure is. Welcome to fatherhood, buddy. Your life will never be the same again."

Alex grinned and looked down at Grace. "I'm looking forward to the change."

Seth couldn't move for a moment. Brad had a son, and now Alex was going to be a father. His two best friends were living the life he'd wanted so desperately for himself—a family where he could be the kind of father he'd always wanted to have. The kind he knew nothing about until Dan Lattimer had come into his life.

He swallowed and walked over to Alex. "Congratulations. You're going to make an awesome father."

Alex smiled. "Thanks, Seth. Don't worry. Your time will come."

Seth bit down on his lip and turned away. He glanced at Callie, whose face registered no emotion at all. Before he could say anything, she stepped forward and stretched out her hand to Grace. "I'm so happy for you, Grace. I know you and Alex will make wonderful parents."

"Thank you, Callie," she said.

Callie took a deep breath, glanced back at the table and then to Laura. "I think we left the buns for the burgers inside. I'll go get them while you finish getting the food ready out here."

Seth watched as she turned and hurried into the house. He still couldn't figure out the look that had passed across her face when he was holding Mark or the way she had reacted to Alex and Grace's announcement.

Alex had told him his time for fatherhood would come, but would it, really? He closed his eyes for a moment, and for the first time in two years let himself give in to the thoughts he'd tried—and failed—to keep at bay.

He needed to accept the truth. He was never

going to be a father because he was never going to find a woman he could love enough to marry and build a family with. Not after Callie. She was the one he wanted, and he didn't think that would ever change.

TEN

Callie breathed a sigh of relief when the evening finally came to an end, and she and Seth prepared to leave. Although she liked Laura and Grace, their conversation after Grace's announcement had centered on the upcoming arrival of Grace's baby and the things she needed to do to prepare for the big event. Every word they'd spoken had been like a nail driven into her heart, but of course they had no way of knowing that.

Now as they stood at the front door and thanked Laura and Brad for dinner and the wonderful evening, Grace stepped onto the porch with them and touched Callie's arm. "I understand what you're going through with your uncle right now, and Alex and I are praying for both of you."

"Thank you."

"My father was injured in a drive-by shooting about two years ago. He lived, but he's confined to a wheelchair. Prayer has become a very important aspect of our everyday life, and I wanted you to know you're in ours. And on our church's prayer list, too."

Callie's eyebrows arched. "Oh, I didn't know you attend church."

Grace laughed. "Yes. Brad and Laura and Seth and his mother go to church with us. We'd love for you to come while you're in town."

Callie shook her head. "Thanks for the invitation, but I doubt if I'll be able to come. I never have attended church much."

Grace smiled. "If you change your mind, come along. We have a great time there."

"I will, and thanks again for the wonderful evening."

Behind her Seth made his parting remarks to his friends while she hurried toward the car. Once inside, she settled back in the seat and pulled the seat belt around her. Within minutes Seth rejoined her and started the car.

As they pulled out into the dark streets that seemed almost empty with the sparse traffic tonight, Seth glanced her way. "I heard Grace invite you to church. Would you like to go with Mom and me in the morning?"

"No, thanks. I think I'll go to the hospital and spend the day there."

He didn't say anything for a moment, then he

exhaled. "Callie, you know my friends aren't the only ones who are praying for Dan. He's in my prayers all the time."

"I know, Seth, but you know I've never been on very friendly terms with God."

"You do believe in Him, don't you?"

"Of course I believe in Him. I believe He created this beautiful world we live in, but I don't understand why He lets bad things happen. When I was a child and found out my mother was sick, I prayed that God would save her. Surely a caring God wouldn't take a father and a mother away from a young girl, but He did. I knew then He didn't care about me."

"But you're wrong, Callie. He did care about you."

She swiveled in her seat and faced him. "And how did He show that?"

"He gave you Dan to take care of you. An uncaring God would have abandoned you, but God loved you so much He gave you an uncle who loved you more than his own life. I think he proved that when he shoved your head down to keep you from getting shot."

Callie stared out the windshield and thought about what Seth had said. His words made sense, but she still wasn't convinced. The memory of the afternoon she'd sat in a doctor's office two years ago and heard the devastating news that would shatter her life returned. She closed her eyes, but his words still rang in her mind.

"Miss Lattimer, I'm sorry, but the tests show that great amounts of scar tissue have developed from the surgeries you had as a child when your bicycle was struck by a car. It appears your fallopian tubes are blocked, which will prevent you from ever being able to have children."

She blinked back the tears and sniffed. "Does God answer all your prayers, Seth?"

"Yes."

She jerked her head around and stared at him. "He does?"

He nodded. "He either answers it with yes or no. The no answers are the hardest to take, but He's always there to get me through the tough times. Later on I see that He only had my best interests at heart."

Callie gave a grunt of disgust. "Unfortunately, every time He says no to me it doesn't seem to be in my best interest."

"Yeah, I've had that happen, too. All I can do is keep being faithful, and know it will all work out in the end." Seth let his gaze drift over her face, and in the light from the dashboard panel she saw the hurt in his eyes she'd first witnessed two years ago. She knew what he was referring to, but she turned her head away and didn't say a word.

Her lips trembled, and she bit down on them and willed the tears in her eyes to go away. The chemistry between them was starting to make itself known again, and she couldn't let that happen. She'd given Seth his freedom so he could have the life he wanted. She wasn't about to do anything now to change that. The best thing she could do was get out of Memphis fast.

"I've been thinking," she said without turning to face him."

"About what?" he asked.

"I think we need to speed up this investigation. So I've decided I'm going to go to the Midtown Mission Monday and volunteer my services."

The car swerved, and he jerked the wheel to bring the car back into its lane. "You'll do nothing of the sort."

She turned a stony gaze on him and spoke with all the authority she could muster. "Yes, I am. It's time we found out who tried to kill Uncle Dan and me. Maybe while I'm there, if I keep my eyes and ears open, I can find out some information that will help us."

"Callie, I don't think…"

She held up her hand. "It's no use, Seth. I'm going to do it whether you like it or not. I want to take Uncle Dan and get out of Memphis, and I can't do it until this case is solved. There's no need for further discussion. I've made my decision."

He started to say something, but instead nodded. "Okay, if that's what you want. I don't want to stand in the way of your getting back to the exciting life you've carved out for yourself in Virginia."

He stared straight ahead and didn't speak again. Callie studied his angry expression out of the corner of her eye and wondered what he would say if he knew how much the words she's just spoken had cost her. She had to put that out of her mind, though.

Right now she needed to concentrate on whether or not there was something at the Midtown Mission that would lead her to the people who'd tried to kill her and her uncle. And she intended to start Monday.

Seth didn't like it a bit. Callie had no business going undercover at Midtown Mission. Truthfully, he didn't know if there was anything unlawful or dangerous going on there, but he didn't like her putting herself at risk just in case she did find suspicious activity. He'd tried to speak to her about it several times, but she'd dismissed his concerns.

Now on Monday afternoon as they sat in the parking lot, he tried once more to convince her to give up this idea and go back to his house. "I think you're taking too much of a risk, Callie," he said for perhaps the fifth time.

She shook her head. "You might as well give up, Seth. I've made up my mind. I'm glad Mrs. Tipton suggested I come help serve the dinner meal. That way I'll only be here for a few hours, and you're going to be around the corner sitting in your car. I have my cell phone, and I'll call you if I see anything suspicious."

He swiveled in his seat and stared at her. "Do you promise you'll call if there's the least hint of any trouble?"

"I will."

He rubbed the back of his neck and exhaled. "Very well, then. Go on. Remember, I'll only be a block away if you need me."

She laughed and climbed out of the car. When she was outside, she leaned down and stared back inside at him. "Don't worry. Everything is going to be fine."

"I hope you're right."

He watched as she walked from the parking lot and weaved her way through the homeless men and women who'd already gathered outside the mission in hopes of getting a warm meal and a bed for the night. He said a quick prayer for Callie's safety before he started the car and drove down the street. He pulled to a stop around the corner just out of sight of the mission and parked beside the curb. Now came the hard part. Waiting. He'd never liked stake-outs, but with Callie involved this might be the worst one he'd ever endured.

There had to be a connection among the Midtown Mission, A.D.A. Abby Dalton, Carlos Allen and the attempts on Dan's and Callie's lives. Maybe Callie could find something that linked everything together.

He reached for his cell phone to call her and ask if everything was all right so far, but he shook his head and pulled his hand back. No need to call attention to her right away. If she had stepped into a dangerous place at Midtown Mission, there was nothing he could do right now except wait and see what happened in the next few hours.

Callie could hardly believe how quickly the time had passed since she first entered the mission. Mrs. Tipton had assigned her right away to work with Peggy Hubbard, the woman she and Seth had spoken to when they visited the mission a few days ago. For the next few hours she worked in the kitchen with Peggy and the other cooks as they prepared the evening meal.

Now with all the tables filled, men and women bent over their plates and shoveled food into their mouths. No one spoke as they ate, and the only sound in the room was of forks and spoons scraping against the dishes.

Callie had known for years that American cities were filled with unfortunate homeless people, but she'd never been so close to any of them before. Even under the dirt and grime on their bodies, she realized these were still human beings, each with a different story. She wondered what some of them were.

She carried a coffeepot as she walked up and down the tables and stopped every once in a while to refill a cup. A mumbled thank-you, no eye contact, was all she received for her service until she stopped beside a man who glanced up at her after she'd poured coffee into his cup.

"Thank you." His smile revealed straight, white teeth that appeared particularly bright against the backdrop of his chocolate-colored skin.

Callie returned his smile. "You're welcome."

He tilted his head and studied her for a moment. "You're new here."

"This is my first time to volunteer. My name is Callie."

"It's good to have you here, Callie. I'm Herman. Herman Miller. But my friends all call me Champ."

Callie's gaze raked the gaunt figure in the faded pants and shirt that seemed to hang on his small frame. "Champ?"

He chuckled. "Yeah. It's a holdover from my Golden Gloves days." He glanced down at his plate. "But I expect a pretty lady like you don't have no time to hear about that."

Callie shook her head. A man next to Herman picked up his empty plate and rose to his feet. When he'd walked away, Callie dropped down in the chair, set her coffeepot on the table and smiled at Herman. "No, you're wrong. I'd love to hear your story."

He glanced around the room. "Everybody here got a story, and ev'ry one of them is just about alike. Mine ain't much different."

"Then tell me."

He took a drink of coffee and stared at the cup when he set it back on the table. A faraway look settled in his eyes, and Callie wondered what thoughts were running through his mind. "Yeah, I used to box in the Golden Gloves. Thought I'd make it to the big leagues, but that wasn't to be. Vietnam got in the way and ended that dream."

"I'm sorry."

He shook his head. "No need to feel bad. I came home in one piece. A lot of guys didn't.

When I got back, all I wanted was a little neighborhood grocery store. I worked hard and I finally got it. Things were going good until my wife died, and I was alone."

"So you had no children?"

"One son, but he took off. Don't know where he is. He didn't want nothing to do with that little grocery store, but I loved it. It was all I had. Then these guys came by, and all that changed."

Callie straightened in her chair. "How did it change?"

"At first, they sweet-talked me, told me they were gonna take care of me, offer me protection from what might happen to an old man trying to run a business by himself. I told them I didn't need no protection, but they said I didn't have a choice. I had to pay them every week if I wanted to stay in business."

"So what did you do?"

"I started to pay them, but it was never enough. They kept raising the price. When it got so much I couldn't pay, I told them I was through. I wasn't making enough money to live on. That night I woke up in my apartment that was over the store, and I smelled smoke. I was lucky to get out of the building alive, but everything I owned burned in the fire that night. I'd been short on money from making those 'protection payments,' and I'd gotten behind on paying my insurance. At my age nobody wanted to hire me, and I had nowhere to live. Next thing I know I'm on the streets and sleeping on a concrete floor in a deserted warehouse most nights."

Callie's heart ached for the man, and tears stood in her eyes. She reached out and squeezed Herman's arm. "I am so sorry for what happened to you, Herman."

His eyes sparkled for a moment, and he smiled. "Champ. I told you my friends call me Champ, and you're the first friend I've made in a long time." He looked down at his plate and cleared his throat. "Now if you don't mind, I need to finish eating. They gonna start drawing names for tonight's beds in a little while, and I'd like to get one. It sure would be nice to have one night on a mattress instead of a cardboard box on a concrete floor."

"Of course." Callie pushed to her feet and looked toward the kitchen. Peggy stood just inside the dining room, watching her. She had her arms crossed over her chest, and a frown creased her face. She shook her head, and Callie felt the unspoken reprimand for slacking off on her responsibilities vibrate through her body to the tips of her toes. She took a deep breath and glanced down at Herman, who had shifted his attention back to the food on his plate. "Would you like another cup of coffee before I move on?"

"No, ma'am. I'm fine, but thanks."

Callie moved down the table to the next man, but she couldn't resist glancing back at Herman, who hadn't looked her way again. Something in the slump of his shoulders and the resigned tone of his words pierced her heart, and she wondered what happened to people that ended up on the streets with no hope. She shook the thought from her head and walked toward the kitchen to refill her now-empty coffeepot.

Peggy waited for her just inside the door. "You don't need to talk to the people who come in here."

The statement surprised Callie, and she frowned. "Why not? I thought the mission was here to help these people."

"It is. But our goal is to meet their physical needs. A meal, a bed for the night, a place to get a shower. Those types of things."

"I don't understand. What about offering them hope or encouragement? Don't you want them to escape the way they're living?"

"Of course we do, but that's not going to happen for most of them. Only a handful will be able to escape their lives on the street."

"You have no way of knowing which ones will escape. In the meantime, why shouldn't you offer kindness and compassion to the ones who come in here?"

"Because they'll want to start spilling the sordid details of their lives. Before you know it you'll be sucked in and feeling sorry for them. Then they'll hit you up for money. I should know. It's happened to me plenty of times."

Callie debated how to respond to Peggy. Evidently, something had happened in her past that influenced her opinion of the people the mission served. Callie hoped she never became too jaded to be willing to reach out to other people. After a moment she nodded. "I'm sorry you've had some bad experiences. I'll keep that in mind."

Peggy's features softened, and she pulled up the corner of her apron and wiped at the perspiration on her forehead. "I'm only telling you this for your own good, Callie."

"Thank you for doing that." Callie smiled and walked over to the big coffee urn across the kitchen. When she'd refilled her pot, she turned and headed back into the dining room.

She had only gotten to the kitchen door when the door that led from the sidewalk outside into the dining room opened, and Marty Weaver stepped into the room. Surprised at seeing him there, she took a step back into the kitchen and watched.

He didn't move for a moment. He stood there,

his arms crossed over his chest, and let his gaze drift over the men and women still eating their dinner. She inched farther back into the kitchen, but he didn't appear to notice her. Her heart beat a little faster when his gaze came to a stop on Herman Miller. The man appeared oblivious to the policeman's presence for a few seconds, then he looked up.

Herman's body slowly stiffened, and his mouth dropped open. He didn't break eye contact with the officer as he laid his fork down on his plate. Then he rose and picked up his still half-filled plate and hurried across the room to the garbage can where he dumped the remaining food. He gave one last glance at the imposing figure just inside the front door before he turned and exited the room through a side door that led outside.

Marty Weaver watched him go before he left and closed the door behind him. Callie set the coffeepot down and ran out the side door that led to the parking lot. Herman was nowhere to be seen, and she rushed to the front of the building. She caught sight of him pushing a shopping cart down the sidewalk, away from the mission.

"Herman," she called out. "Wait!" He didn't look around, and she called again. "Champ!"

He stopped, slowly turned and waited for her

to catch up to him. When she stopped beside him, he gave her a quizzical look. "Yes, ma'am?"

"Why are you leaving? I thought you were going to try to get a bed."

He shook his head. "Not tonight. I guess I'll go back to the warehouse. Maybe we'll meet again."

"I'll be back tomorrow. I'll see you then." But he was already walking away from her, and he gave no indication he'd heard her words.

After a moment, Callie sighed and turned back to the shelter. Herman's story kept ringing in her mind. She'd overheard Seth and his partners discussing a racketeering case they were working on where money was being extorted from small-business owners. Could Herman be one of the victims of the ring? She'd have to discuss this with Seth right away.

She'd only taken a few steps when she stopped. Why had Herman appeared to be so frightened when Marty Weaver had walked into the mission? This wasn't the first time the policeman's unexpected presence had made her suspicious of his motives.

From the way it was beginning to look, Marty Weaver just might be the person with the answers about everything she'd experienced since she'd arrived in Memphis. If he was, she and Seth needed to be careful and proceed with

ELEVEN

Seth glanced at his watch and sighed. Callie had only been inside the mission for a few hours, but the time had seemed to drag for him. He squirmed and tried to settle into a more comfortable position, but he'd never liked the long hours in a car during stakeouts. Today was no exception.

He'd occupied his time by studying Dan's notebook, but nothing new had jumped out at him. Maybe he'd looked at it too much in the past. He was about to close the book when a notation at the bottom of one of the pages caught his attention.

He pulled the book closer and studied Dan's handwriting on the page in the waning daylight. According to the entry Dan had sent a sample of Hope's DNA to the Tennessee Bureau of Investigation over two years ago. There was nothing else written down to indicate that there had ever been a match.

Seth exhaled a deep breath and shook his head. "Maybe she didn't have any family," he murmured.

He pulled his cell phone from his pocket and was about to place a call when the passenger-side door opened, and Callie climbed in. "Who are you calling?" she asked.

He pointed to the bottom of the notebook page. "I just saw where Dan had made this notation. He never told me he'd sent Hope's DNA to the TBI lab. I know the data entry clerk there. I was going to call her and ask about it."

Callie pointed to the clock on the dash. "Will the office still be open this late?"

Seth sighed and shook his head. "I guess not. I'll get in touch with her tomorrow." He slipped the phone into his pocket, glanced at her and frowned. "Are you okay?"

She took a deep breath. "I'm fine, just glad to see you," she said.

The scared look on her face, coupled with her words, made the hairs on the back of his neck stand up. He straightened in his seat. "I can tell it's something else. Did something happen while you were at the shelter?"

"It may be nothing, but I can't shake the feeling that I just witnessed something sinister." She quickly told him of her meeting with Herman and how he'd left when Marty Weaver came into the dining room. When she'd finished, she leaned closer to Seth. "It was as if Marty scared him for some reason. He couldn't get out of there fast enough. Even gave up the chance to have his name drawn for a bed, which he'd told me he was looking forward to."

Seth rubbed the back of his neck and frowned. "I agree it sounds suspicious, but the homeless are often afraid of the police. Then again, you may have just stumbled on somebody that might be able to help us on the racketeering case we've been working on. I need to talk to Herman. Where was he going for the night?"

"He said he slept in an abandoned warehouse, but I don't know where."

"I have a friend who patrols the area where a lot of the homeless sleep. I'll call him and see if he knows Herman. If he does, maybe he can keep an eye on him tonight."

"That would make me feel a lot better."

Seth punched in the number and gave a slight nod to Callie when his friend answered. "Max Prince speaking."

"Hey, Max, this is Seth Dawtry. Glad I was able to catch you."

"Seth, good to hear from you. What can I do for you?"

"I've been working on an unsolved murder related to a racketeering case for a while, and I just got a lead that a homeless man named Herman Miller may have some information. Do you know him?"

"Yeah, we call him Champ. He hangs out in an abandoned warehouse down near the river. We've been trying to pass the word through the homeless community that the building is scheduled to be demolished in thirty days, but there are a lot of people who have their spaces set up there. They don't want to move."

"Do you plan to check on that building tonight?"

"It depends on how busy we get with other calls coming in, but we'll try to get by there."

"Would you check on Herman for me? Tell him I really need to talk to him."

"I'll do it. I go off duty at seven in the morning. I'll give you a call before I go home."

"Thanks, Max. Talk to you later."

Seth ended the call and turned to Callie. "He'll check on Herman and call me in the morning."

Callie smiled at him. "Thanks, Seth. My heart went out to that man as I listened to him tell his life story." She closed her eyes and took a deep breath. "Maybe today has been more productive than we expected. I met a man who may give you a lead on that racketeering case, and you found Uncle Dan's note about sending Hope's

DNA to the TBI lab. Wouldn't it be wonderful if we could solve both cases?"

Seth chuckled and started the car. "It would be, but don't get your hopes up. I've been disappointed many times when I thought I was onto a hot lead, and it turned out to be nothing. It takes a lot of patience and time to solve most of our cases."

"I know. Uncle Dan has told me that many times. But I think twenty-five years is long enough for Hope's case to go unsolved. I'd love to be able to tell him it's solved when he wakes up from his coma."

Seth darted a glance at her profile and smiled. He recognized the determined jut of her jaw and knew she shared the tenacity of her uncle. She wouldn't give up until she'd found out Hope's identity. "I want that, too. But in the meantime, Mom called and said she's going to be out for the evening. Want to do the drive-through at that rib place?"

Callie nodded. "Sounds good to me."

Forty-five minutes later they walked into the kitchen at Seth's home. He set the container with their dinner on the kitchen table and glanced over at Callie, who was already pulling some plates from the cabinets to set the table. He watched her work for a moment, and his heart twisted in his chest.

A feeling of déjà vu settled over him, and he closed his eyes. How many times had they spent evenings together here or at Dan's home, working together to get a meal on the table? He wished he had known then how special those times were to become to him and how quickly they could vanish without a word of warning.

She glanced up at him, and their eyes locked. He stared at her for a moment before he turned away. "I'll get some soft drinks out of the fridge."

"Okay."

He brought two cans to the table. They sat down, and she began to eat. He stared down at his plate for a moment, then he bowed his head and silently offered his thanks for the food God had provided. When he opened his eyes, she was staring at him.

"Is anything the matter?" he asked.

"No."

She dropped her gaze to her plate and began to eat again. He had just raised his fork to his mouth when his phone rang. He pulled it from his pocket and stared at the displayed number. "It's Max Prince."

Callie put her fork down and sat up straighter. "Maybe he's seen Herman."

Seth pulled the phone to his ear. "Hello."

"Seth, this is Max. I'm afraid I've got some bad news for you."

Seth's heart dropped to the pit of his stomach. "What is it?"

"We answered a call that the body of a homeless man had been found near the abandoned warehouse I was telling you about earlier. When we got there, I recognized the victim. It was Herman Miller. He'd been shot."

Seth closed his eyes and shook his head. "Oh, no. Do you have any suspects?"

"No. As usual with the street people, nobody heard or saw anything. Thought I'd let you know."

"Thanks, Max. I'll talk to you later."

He disconnected the call and sat there staring at his phone. Callie leaned forward and touched his arm. "What did Max say?"

He took a deep breath and looked into her eyes. "They found Herman shot to death near the warehouse where he slept."

She shook her head, and tears began to trail down her cheeks. "No, that can't be," she whispered. "I just talked to him a few hours ago. Why would anybody kill him?"

"Maybe he knew something they didn't want him telling anyone."

She picked up her napkin and wiped at her

eyes. "Do you think he might have been killed because he talked to me?"

Seth shook his head. "I don't think a conversation that lasted only a few minutes would have been a reason for him to be killed. He didn't divulge any secrets, did he? Like who burned his shop down?"

"No."

"Then I doubt if it did."

She picked up her plate, walked to the trash can and dumped her food. When she set her plate in the sink, she gripped the side of the counter and stared down for a few moments. "Hope and Herman, two people I'd never heard of before coming back to Memphis, and my heart is breaking for both of them. It's so unfair. What harm could a young woman and an old man do to anyone?" She turned back to Seth. "Do you think we'll ever find out the truth about either one of their deaths?"

Seth wanted to reassure her, and he knew that's what she wanted, too. But he had worked the Cold Case Unit long enough to know that some cases were never solved, and some families never received the answers they wanted. "I don't know, Callie."

She brushed at her eyes with her fingers and

nodded. "I think I'll go upstairs. Tell your mother good-night for me when she comes home."

Before he could say anything, she hurried from the room and ran up the stairs. A few minutes later he heard her bedroom door close, and he sat back down at the table. He glanced down at his plate and discovered his hunger had disappeared.

He pushed the plate away, rose to his feet and walked out the door into the backyard. With his hands thrust in his pockets he stood underneath the night sky and gazed up at the stars twinkling above. Pictures flashed like a slideshow in his mind—a homeless man whose face he couldn't see as he walked down the street pushing his cart; Dan lying in a coma, still in a hospital bed; Hope's lifeless body on a medical examiner's table and Callie walking away from him two years ago. So much tragedy. All of it had impacted his life, and he didn't have a clue what he could do about any of it. Suddenly he felt alone. "God, have You left me? Why can't I find the answers I need?"

Than an answer welled up in his heart as a Bible verse came to mind. *Lo, I am with you always, even to the end of the world.*

Seth closed his eyes and smiled. The answers were going to come, and from the way his heart was beating, he didn't think he had too long to wait.

Seth still felt hopeful the next afternoon when he delivered Callie to the front door of the Midtown Mission. He fought back the uneasy feeling he had about her continued presence at the shelter.

"Be careful," he warned for perhaps the fourth time since they left home.

She laughed and opened the door. "I will, Seth. Don't worry. You're going to be just around the corner. If I need you, I'll call."

"Be sure and do that," he said as she closed the door and walked toward the shelter entrance.

He waited for a few moments to see if she looked back out the door. When she didn't, he shook his head and drove down the street. Why was he so jumpy today? Ever since last night he'd had this thought that it wasn't going to be long before he had the answers he'd been helping Dan try to find for years.

He pulled around the corner, parked in the same spot from the previous day, and settled back to wait for Callie to return. The clock on the dash displayed 4:50 p.m., and he suddenly remembered he'd forgotten to call the data entry clerk at the TBI office today to ask if there'd been any hits on Hope's DNA.

The office closed at 5:00, but he might be able to catch her before she left for home. He dialed the number and waited, but there was no answer. When it went to voice mail, he left his message.

"Mrs. Riley, this is Seth Dawtry with the Memphis PD. I need some information on a cold case we're investigating. Judge Dan Lattimer entered the DNA of a young woman he called Hope in the database some time ago. I need to know if there has ever been a hit or anyone who contacted you about it." He rattled off his phone number. "Please call me at this number to let me know. Thank you."

He disconnected the call and stuck his cell phone back in his pocket. Then he settled back in his seat, but he couldn't get comfortable. He squirmed this way and that, trying to relax, but it was no use.

He couldn't shake the feeling that something was about to happen, and it was going to be bad.

Callie's gaze drifted over the shelter's dining room where the homeless men and women sat, hoping their name would be called for a bed, and tears welled up in her eyes. Even though she'd only met Herman once, she could feel his absence tonight.

Callie moved among those eating and poured coffee for those who still had cups. She emptied

the last of the pot into the cup of a stoop-shoul-
dered man with matted gray hair. He looked
up at her with a toothless smile, and her heart
melted. Herman's face flashed in her mind, and
she blinked back tears. She returned the man's
smile and headed back to the kitchen for a refill.

Just as she stepped from the room, she heard
the front door open and glanced over her shoulder. Assistant District Attorney Abby Dalton
walked into the room, wrinkled up her nose
and strode down the hallway toward Dorothy
Tipton's office.

Callie set the coffeepot on the kitchen counter
and smiled at Peggy, who had just taken a tray
of rolls out of the oven. "I have to go the ladies'
room, Peggy. I'll be back in a few minutes."

Peggy frowned. "Well, don't be gone long.
I'm short-staffed tonight, and I'm getting
ready to draw the names for beds." She rolled
her eyes. "You'd think Dorothy would help me
when somebody's out. But no, her ladyship can't
be bothered to do any of the real work around
here."

Callie's eyebrows arched at the snide tone
of Peggy's words, but she suddenly realized
she had never seen Mrs. Tipton do any physical work in the shelter, either. "I won't be gone
long."

Callie walked from the kitchen and hurried

down the hallway that led to Dorothy's office. She stopped outside the closed door and was about to lean closer to see if she could hear anything from the other side when she glanced over her shoulder and saw the homeless man she'd poured coffee for a few minutes earlier standing at the entrance to the hallway and staring at her from the dining room. She smiled at him and continued to the ladies' room.

When she came back out, she looked toward the dining room, but the man no longer stood there. She debated whether or not to stop and try to hear what was being said inside the office and had almost convinced herself to move on when a sharp "No!" rang out from inside.

She stopped and inched closer to the door. Loud voices penetrated the thin, wooden panels, and Callie strained to hear what was being said on the other side.

"I'm through, I tell you. I'm not making any more deals with you and your friends. From now on, you're on your own." Callie recognized the nasal sound of Abby Dalton's voice.

"You listen to me," Dorothy's voice boomed, "you'll do what you're told. There are a lot of guys you've sent to prison who would just love the opportunity to shut you up for good."

"Y-you can't threaten me. I'm an assistant district attorney."

Dorothy laughed. "And how long do you think that would last if your boss knew all the kickbacks you've taken to let felons off the hook? You might find yourself sharing a cell with somebody who really has it in for you."

"And some of those friends I've made by letting them off might like the opportunity to shut up a loudmouth like you, Dorothy. So if you know what's good for you, you'll stop telling me what to do. Now I'm leaving and I want you to tell your friends their little racket is over, and I'm out."

"You're not leaving until I say you can."

Callie pressed her ear against the door as the sounds of a scuffle welled up from inside the office. A chair crashed to the floor. Something made of glass shattered. Callie clamped her hand over her mouth. She couldn't believe what she was hearing. She had to call Seth and get him to the shelter as soon as possible.

She pulled her cell phone from her pocket and backed up a step to distance herself from the door. Before she could punch Seth's number in the phone, her foot struck something behind her, and she stopped. A hand clamped down on her shoulder and squeezed hard. Her legs threatened to collapse, and her heart exploded in her chest.

A warm breath fanned her cheek, and a deep voice whispered in her ear. "What do you think you're doing?"

TWELVE

Callie breathed a sigh of relief when she turned and stared into the face of her uncle's best friend and former partner, Captain Anthony Wilson. There was no need to call Seth now. She slipped the phone back into her pocket. "Anthony, what are you doing here?"

He frowned and shook his head. "Checking on you. I ran into Marty Weaver, and he told me he'd come by looking for an informant last night. He said he saw you working here. Why?"

She shook her head. "There's no time to go into that now. Assistant District Attorney Abby Dalton is inside with Dorothy Tipton. They've been yelling and fighting."

"Fighting?"

She pulled him closer to the door. "You've got to get in there right away and arrest them. I heard them talk about all these felons Abby has released to help Dorothy and her friends with some kind of racket."

"You did?" Anthony pulled his gun from his holster. He stepped around Callie. "Stay behind me."

Callie jumped behind Anthony and watched as he turned the knob and pushed the door open. He burst into the room with Callie right behind him. Once inside he reached around her and closed the door. "Okay, ladies. Callie tells me you've been yelling and making some wild accusations in here. Anybody want to tell me what's going on?"

Abby's and Dorothy's mouths dropped open, and they stared in disbelief at Callie. "I don't know what she's talking about," Abby said.

"Neither do I," Dorothy added.

Callie stepped up beside Anthony. "They're lying. You can tell they've been in a fight from the overturned table and the broken glass on the floor. I heard everything they said. They've been working together in some kind of racket. Abby gets a kickback for dropping charges against prisoners so they can work with them. From the way it sounded, you need to arrest them and find out what they're involved in."

Anthony's eyebrows arched. "You don't say."

Callie nodded. "Yes, and when you find out, I'll be glad to testify in court against them."

"You'd do that?" Anthony asked.

Callie frowned. "Of course. Why wouldn't I?"

Anthony sighed. "Because that might prove too unhealthy for you."

"I don't understand."

Anthony turned back to the door and locked it. Then he faced Dorothy and Abby. "I've warned you two before that your catfights were going to cause us a lot of trouble. Now look what you've done. You've left another mess I have to clean up."

Dorothy clasped her hands in front of her. "I'm sorry, Anthony. What are you going to do?"

Callie's mouth dropped open, and she stared from Dorothy to Anthony in disbelief. "She sounds like she knows you, Anthony. What's going on here?"

"Yeah. She knows me all right. She's my cousin." He glared at Dorothy before he turned to Callie. "And you should never have stuck your nose into something that didn't concern you."

Anthony took a step toward Callie, and she backed away. "I don't understand. Why aren't you arresting them?"

"Arrest me? Is that what you were after?" The sharp words from Dorothy startled Callie. Before Callie could move, Dorothy stormed over to stand beside Anthony and raised her hand to slap Callie. "You little sneak. You come down here wanting to help, and all you're doing is spying on us."

Callie threw her hands in front of her face and cowered as Dorothy swung her palm toward her. Before she made contact, Anthony grabbed Dorothy's hand and held it in a tight grip. "There's no need for that, Dorothy. We don't want any more noise in here than we've already had. I'll take care of Callie. You take her cell phone and then get back out front. We need to keep everything operating smoothly in the shelter."

Dorothy took a step closer to Callie, but she grabbed Dorothy's arm when she reached out to take the phone from her pocket. "No, leave me alone."

Anthony snarled. "Be still, or you'll wish you had."

Callie lowered her arm and watched helplessly as Dorothy pulled her phone from her pocket and slipped it into hers. Then she looked back at Anthony. "I'll dispose of the cell phone. What are you going to do now?"

"You just concentrate on keeping everything on track here. If Seth comes looking for Callie, tell him you don't know where she went. Abby and I can take care of Callie."

"Oh, no, not me!" Abby's shrill voice cried out. "I'm going home. I don't want anything to do with what you're planning. From now on, count me out."

Before Abby could move, Anthony was across

the floor and had grabbed her arm with one hand while the other held his gun to her head. "I'm not counting you out of anything. You're in this as deep as any of us, and you'll do what I say if you know what's best."

Tears began to roll down Abby's face. "Please, Anthony. I don't want to have any part in killing somebody."

"Like it or not, you're coming with me."

Callie's body jerked in surprise at the exchange between the two. Anthony, her uncle's best friend, was going to kill her? How could that be? She'd thought of him as a family member since she was a little girl, and now he wanted her dead.

She glanced around the room for a way to escape. With Dorothy and Anthony's attention focused on Abby, they had moved away from her. She had to do something.

Think, Callie, she told herself. *How can you get out of here?* The door. If she could get to it and turn the bolt, she might be able to run down the hallway and out the back exit. Then down the alley and a block over to where Seth waited in a car.

She eased across the floor, reached for the lock's button knob and turned it. To her relief, it made no sound as the bolt slid back into place.

From across the room Abby cried out again, and Anthony slapped her. "Quit your crying."

In one swift movement, Callie pulled the door open, ran into the hall and sprinted toward the exit door at the end of the hallway. She burst through the door into the darkness of the back parking lot where the staff kept their cars and turned to run in the direction where Seth waited.

"Callie, stop!" a loud voice demanded.

She skidded to a stop and whirled to see Marty Weaver standing at the edge of the parking lot with his gun drawn. New fear washed over Callie, and she turned to run. "No!" she screamed and bolted forward.

Too late she realized she had gone the wrong way when she ran from the building. It dawned on her suddenly when she plowed into the four-foot wire fence that ran from the back of the building along the property edge. The driveway into the parking lot lay on the other side of the shelter.

The impact of her collision knocked the breath from her and slammed her to the ground. Then she heard footsteps running toward her. She tried to get up, but her knees screamed with pain.

Marty Weaver dropped down beside her. "Are you all right?"

"No," she shouted. "Get away from me."

He looked over his shoulder. "What's going on, Callie? Is someone after you?"

She frowned and shook her head to clear it of her muddled thoughts. "Aren't you with him?"

"With who?" Marty asked.

Callie pushed up into a sitting position. "With Anthony."

At that moment the back door of the shelter burst open, and Anthony ran into the parking lot. His eyes locked on her and Marty, and he started across the pavement, his gun leveled at them.

"Get away from her, Marty," he said.

Marty rose to his feet and looked from him to Callie, a puzzled expression on his face. "I don't understand. I was only helping her."

Anthony cocked his gun. "I said get away."

Marty took a step toward him, and Callie jumped to her feet. "No, Marty. Don't trust him. He wants to kill me."

Marty's mouth dropped open, and he glanced at her before he looked back at Anthony. Marty raised his gun. "Captain, maybe you should take a step..."

Before he could finish his sentence, two gunshots rang out, and Marty staggered forward before he fell to the ground. Callie screamed and dropped to her knees beside him. Anthony ran to her, grabbed her by the arm and jerked her to her feet. "You shot a police officer, Anthony. How could you do that?"

He tightened his grip and dragged her across the parking lot toward his police car where Abby stood waiting. "Open the door," he growled at her.

Even in the dimly lit parking lot, Callie could see the fear etched in Abby's face as she jerked the door open. Anthony pushed Callie inside and slammed the door. She slid across the seat and reached for the handle on the other door, but she couldn't find it. Then she realized her predicament. She was in the backseat of a police car used for transporting prisoners. Those cars weren't equipped with door handles on the backseat.

The front doors of the car opened, and Anthony slid behind the steering wheel. Abby climbed into the passenger side. Without speaking, he started the car, pulled around the building toward the street and waited for several cars to pass.

Callie glanced out the window and hoped he would turn left. If he did, they would pass the street where Seth sat waiting for her in his car. By some stroke of luck he might be able to see her in the backseat. That is, if he even noticed the car.

Anthony drove the car into the street and turned right.

As they sped down the street away from the shelter, they left behind a wounded Marty Weaver and Seth, the only person who knew she was undercover in the shelter. How long would it be before he checked on her? And what would anybody there tell him?

She stared out the window into the dark night, and her body began to shake with fear. She had no idea where Anthony was taking her, but one thing she did know. He planned to kill her, and at this point she didn't know anything that could stop him from doing just that.

Seth squirmed in the car seat and tried once more to find a comfortable position, but it was no use. His back ached, and the muscles in his legs cramped. Surely Callie would be back soon.

He glanced at the clock and frowned. Eight-fifteen p.m. He didn't realize it had gotten so late. She had only done a three-hour shift last night, and he'd assumed tonight would be the same. What could be keeping her? Maybe he should call her.

He pulled his cell phone from his pocket and was about to punch in her number when his phone rang. He pressed the phone to his ear. "Hello."

"Seth? This is Anne Riley from the TBI office."

"Mrs. Riley, when I left you a message earlier, I thought you had probably gone home for the night. I didn't expect you to call me until tomorrow."

"No, I hadn't gone home. In fact, I'd been away from the office for a doctor's appointment. I came in a little while ago to check my messages, and I got yours. I thought I should call you right away."

Seth straightened in the seat. "Why?"

"It just seemed so strange to me that I would have two calls within a week's time about that DNA sample."

"Somebody else called you? Who was it?"

"Judge Lattimer," she said. "He called almost a week ago."

"And what did you tell him?"

"I checked the records carefully and found nothing. When I told him that there was no record of the DNA being entered for that victim, he became very upset."

Seth frowned. "What happened? Had he thought he entered it, but then he forgot to do it?"

"No. He said he gave it to someone else to

enter for him, and that person said he'd taken care of it."

"Did he say who this person was?"

"No, but he seemed very upset. He said this person was a police officer, and he was going to look into what had happened. Now that I've thought about it, it seems strange that Judge Lattimer was injured later on the day he called me."

Seth felt his pulse quicken. "I think you're right."

"So when I got your message about the same DNA, I called right away. I hope this information has been helpful."

"It has, Mrs. Riley. Thank you for calling."

"You're welcome, Detective. Call me if I can do anything else for you."

"I will."

Seth ended the call and sat there a few moments, thinking about what Mrs. Riley had told him. Who could have betrayed Dan with the DNA evidence? The first name that came to mind was Marty Weaver. For some time Marty's name had seemed to pop into his mind every time he tried to link anybody to this case. Tomorrow he'd have to do some more checking into Marty's background and his recent activities.

His gaze drifted to the clock on the dashboard, and he frowned. What was keeping

Callie? Maybe he needed to go check on her. He had just turned the ignition when sharp reports pierced the quiet night air. Gunshots. And they came from the vicinity of the shelter.

He turned on his blue dashboard light and made a swift U-turn to head around the corner to the mission. The car skidded to a stop at the front door, and he was out the door and running for the entrance before the car came to a complete stop.

He burst into the dining room and was met with a roomful of homeless men and women huddled in their chairs. An old woman stood near the front wall, screaming the same words over and over. "They shootin' people ev'rywhere. They gonna kill us all!"

Peggy had run from the kitchen and was trying to pull the woman toward a chair, but the woman was stronger than she appeared. She struggled from Peggy's grasp and continued her rant.

Seth ran up to her. "Where's Callie?"

Peggy wiped her hand across the perspiration on her forehead. "I don't know," she said. "She went to the ladies' room about fifteen minutes ago, but she hasn't come back yet. And I told her to hurry. I'm short-staffed. We heard shots a few minutes ago, and Sadie thinks somebody's going to come in here and attack us. She's getting everybody upset."

He glanced around the room. "Where is Mrs. Tipton?"

"I don't know. I went back to her office a few minutes ago to get her to help me give out the beds, and she was pulling money out of her desk and stuffing it in a bag. Then she ran past me and out the back door. I heard her car roar out of the parking lot. She usually deals with Sadie, not me. How am I ever going to settle her down?"

Seth headed toward the hallway, but a man with matted gray hair rose from his chair. "I seen Miss Callie."

Seth stopped and faced him. "You did? When?"

He pointed down the hall. "She went down there."

"Did she come back?"

The man shook his head. "Not after that policeman took her in Miss Dorothy's office."

Seth's stomach roiled. "Did you know this policeman?"

He nodded. "He comes here a lot, but I don't know his name."

Seth remembered Callie telling him about Marty's appearance at the shelter the night before. He turned and called out to Peggy, "Did you see Marty Weaver come in here tonight? He's a Memphis police officer."

She shook her head. "No," she grunted as she finally got Sadie settled in a chair. "I haven't seen a policeman come in tonight."

Seth glanced back at the homeless man. "Are you sure you saw a policeman?"

He raised his hand and pointed down the hallway. "He came in the back door. I saw him take Miss Callie in the office."

Seth pulled his gun from his holster, raced down the hallway and skidded to a stop at the open door to Dorothy Tipton's office. A quick glance around the empty room that showed clear signs of a fight confirmed his fear that something bad had happened to Callie.

He rushed to the exit at the end of the hallway and stopped. Not knowing what awaited him outside, he pushed the door open slowly before he stepped into the empty parking lot. His gaze swept the area, and his hand holding the gun dipped. A soft moan drifted on the night air, and he jerked his gun back into firing position.

"Help me," the voice said. Seth squinted into the darkness and made out the crumpled form of someone on the ground.

He inched forward, both hands grasping the gun he held in front of him, and gasped when he recognized Marty Weaver on the ground. Even in the dim light of the parking lot, he could see blood pooling around Marty's body. Seth rushed to him and knelt down.

"Marty! Can you hear me?"

Marty didn't respond. Seth pulled his cell phone out and punched in 911. When the operator answered, he identified himself and his location. "We have an officer down. He's been shot. I need backup and an ambulance right away."

"They're on the way," came the quick response.

Seth shoved the phone back in his pocket and leaned down over Marty. "Marty, it's Seth Dawtry. Can you open your eyes?"

Marty's lips moved, and a low groan rumbled in his throat. "H-he t-took h-her," he whispered.

Fear gripped Seth's heart, and he leaned closer to Marty. "Who?"

Marty's eyes fluttered open, and he stared up into Seth's face. "Captain W-Wilson. Sh-shot me. He and Abby D-Dalton put C-Callie in his police car."

"Abby Dalton?" Things were getting crazier by the moment. Seth frowned and shook his head in disbelief. "I don't understand. Why would Anthony and Abby do something like that?"

Marty grimaced, grabbed the front of Seth's shirt in his hand and clutched the material between his fingers. "Gonna k-kill her. You've got t-to save her."

The back door of the shelter burst open, and Peggy ran into the parking lot. "What's going on out here?" she demanded as she ran to where Marty lay. When she stopped beside Seth, she stared openmouthed down at Marty and then looked back up at Seth. "How badly is he hurt?"

Sirens sounded in the distance, and Seth rose to his feet. "An ambulance and the police are on their way here. Lieutenant Weaver says Captain Wilson shot him. Have you seen the captain tonight?"

Peggy shook her head, "No, but I hardly ever see him when he comes here."

"So he comes here a lot?"

Peggy nodded. "Yes. He's Dorothy's cousin. He usually parks out here and comes in the back door to her office."

"Did you see Abby Dalton?"

"Yes. She came in right before Callie left the kitchen to go to the ladies' room." She looked around the empty parking lot. "Where is Callie?"

The back door opened, and the homeless man who had told Seth he'd seen Callie stuck his head outside. "Miss Peggy, Sadie's gettin' real upset. We need you back inside."

"Go take care of the people inside, Peggy,

but don't leave the shelter or allow anyone in there to go, either. We may need to ask all of you some questions."

Peggy bit down on her lip, but nodded in understanding before she ran to the door. When she'd disappeared inside, Seth knelt beside Marty again. "Our guys should be here any minute, Marty. Just take it easy until they do."

Marty licked his lips and struggled to speak. "I t-tried to help h-her."

"I know. Now lie still."

He closed his eyes and shook his head. "Carlos Allen…"

Seth's heart thudded, and he leaned closer. "What about Carlos?"

"N-never understood who sh-shot first. Shot c-came from b-behind me, l-like from the vacant h-house across the street."

Seth could hardly breathe, his heart was beating so fast. "You didn't think it was your men? You thought it was somebody who wasn't supposed to be there?"

Marty's chin dipped toward his chest in what Seth thought was a weak nod. "Didn't know why Captain Wilson showed up. Nobody but my guys and you knew about the stakeout."

The reason for Marty's defense of his men's actions that night suddenly dawned on Seth.

Marty had suspected someone else who didn't want Carlos taken alive had fired that first shot.

"So you suspected Anthony shot Carlos?"

"Yes."

Seth remembered Callie telling him about how Herman had left the shelter when he saw Marty at the front door. "Why was Herman Miller afraid of you?"

"Wasn't afraid of m-me. W-was one of my informants. When h-he left the shelter last night, he w-was scared. Told me he s-saw Anthony and another man beat up the owner of a d-dry cleaners. He was g-gonna take me to t-talk to the man, but H-Herman was…"

"Was killed, I know," Seth filled in.

"F-followed Anthony tonight to s-see if I could find out anything." He coughed and grabbed his side. "But I c-couldn't save Callie."

The screech of brakes and the wail of sirens outside the shelter alerted Seth that backup had arrived. "Our guys are here, Marty. They'll take care of you, and I'll find Callie."

Marty grabbed his arm before he could move away. "Hurry, Seth. Anthony is g-going to kill her, too."

Before Seth could respond, the back door of the shelter opened, and two EMTs followed by two police officers ran into the parking lot. Seth backed away so they could begin their work on Marty. He motioned to the police officers. "Come with me."

They followed as he turned and ran back into the shelter. They had to find Callie. But how? Dorothy Tipton! Right now she was the only person he could think of who might have the information he needed. Maybe she knew where Anthony would have taken her.

They slid to a stop in the dining room where Peggy had finally calmed the screaming Sadie. An additional four uniformed police officers ran in the front door as he entered and joined them.

"What's going on, Detective?" one of the men who'd followed him back inside asked.

"Lieutenant Marty Weaver has been shot by Captain Anthony Wilson. The captain has also abducted Judge Lattimer's niece. We've got to find him before he kills her." He faced Peggy. "Do you know where Dorothy Tipton went?"

She shook her head. "All I know is I heard her car leave, and she was in a hurry. She might have been going home."

"Where does she live?"

"She lives in a small cottage behind Anthony's house."

Seth turned to the two men who'd been outside with him. "You two stay here. See that Lieutenant Weaver is taken care of and get the crime scene people down here. Get a BOLO out for Captain Wilson's car and tell them to approach him with caution. He's armed and dangerous. He'll have two women with him. One is his abductee, Callie Lattimer. The other is his accomplice, Assistant District Attorney Abby Dalton. The rest of you men follow me to his house. We need to try to find his cousin and see if she has any idea where he might have taken Callie."

"We're with you," one of the officers said.

Seth gave a curt nod and ran toward the door. Within minutes he was roaring down the street, his blue lights flashing and his siren wailing. Two police cars trailed him with their lights flashing as they weaved through traffic.

Seth gripped the steering wheel and gritted his teeth. If anything happened to Callie he would never forgive himself. "God," he whispered, "please don't let her die. I still love her so much. Give me one more chance with her."

He blinked the tears from his eyes and tried to concentrate on his driving. All he could think of, though, was Callie and how she was at the mercy of someone intent on ending her life. He had to find her before Anthony killed her.

THIRTEEN

The first thing Seth noticed when he roared into the driveway at Anthony Wilson's home was that no lights burned in the house. That shouldn't surprise him. He hadn't expected Anthony to bring Callie here. He drove around the house and came to a stop at the small cottage at the back of the property. A black car was parked in front, and lights burned in nearly every room.

Seth jumped from the car, his gun drawn, almost before the car engine had died. Behind him he heard the other officers getting out of their cars. He ran over to the black car, placed his hand on the hood and glanced over his shoulder.

"The hood's warm. This car hasn't been here long."

The other officers pulled their guns, and one pointed to the rear of the house. "My partner and I will go around back and make sure she doesn't try to leave that way."

Seth nodded, and the other two officers followed him as he hurried to the front door and knocked. "Mrs. Tipton," he called out, "we're with the Memphis Police Department. Open your door."

No one answered.

After a moment he knocked again. "There's no escaping us, Mrs. Tipton. It'll go better for you if you talk to us."

The doorknob turned, and the door slowly opened. Dorothy Tipton, her face pale and her body trembling, stood there staring at them. "What do you want?"

"We need to talk with you. May we come in?"

She didn't move for a moment, then she sighed and stepped aside. Seth and the two officers brushed past her into the house. They stopped in the entry hall and waited for her to close the door.

"What do you want?" she asked.

"We need some information. Your cousin Anthony Wilson has wounded an officer and abducted Callie Lattimer. We need to know where he's taken her."

She shook her head. "What makes you think I'd know anything about that?"

Seth swallowed and struggled to control his

anger. He glared at her and took a step nearer. "Look, I don't have time to play games. You ran right by a wounded officer when you drove off from the shelter. If nothing else, I can arrest you right now for being an accessory to attempted murder. If he dies, it'll be murder. Add your role in Callie's death to that, and you're looking at the rest of your life in prison. The thing for you to do is to try to make the best deal for yourself that you can. Things will go a lot easier with you if you tell us where Anthony has taken Callie."

Dorothy's lips trembled, and a tear slipped down her cheek. "I didn't have anything to do with that. Callie overheard Abby and me talking, and she was going to the police. Anthony said he'd take care of her."

Seth gritted his teeth. "Your chances of making a deal are getting slimmer by the minute. Save yourself, Dorothy. Where is Anthony?"

He could see the indecision written on her face as she struggled to decide what to do. After a moment she burst into tears. Her body shook, and she put her hands on either side of her face and pressed them down hard.

"All right, I'll tell you. He has a farm his parents left him. He probably took her there. It's where he buried that woman's car after he killed her."

"What woman?"

"The one whose family Judge Lattimer wanted to find."

Stunned, Seth blinked. "Hope? He killed Hope?"

Dorothy shrugged. "I don't know. Was that her name? She was the one from years ago."

Seth could hardly believe what he'd just heard. Anthony had killed Hope? He pushed the thoughts aside. Right now he had to find Callie. "Where is this farm?"

"It's north of town. Turn off on the old levee road and drive toward the river. You'll see it. It has a bulldozer sitting in the yard."

Seth turned to two of the officers. "Take Mrs. Tipton downtown and hold her for questioning until we know what the charges are going to be. You other two follow me to the farm."

"Detective, isn't that out of our jurisdiction?" one of the officers asked.

Seth nodded. "It is. I'll call the Shelby County Sheriff's office on the way and have them meet us there."

He ran out of the house and jumped in his car. The two officers who were to accompany him did the same, and they sped from the house toward Anthony Wilson's farm.

The streetlights seemed to fly by as Seth zoomed along the Memphis streets. The nearer they came to the edge of town the harder he pushed the accelerator to the floorboard. He couldn't let Callie die. He had to make it in time.

Callie sat in the back of the car and stared out the window. Although she hadn't lived in Memphis in several years, she still knew the city well. For the past few minutes, though, she'd begun to grow uneasy. They'd left the busy streets of the city, driven well past the city limits and now rode through a sparsely populated area on the northern edge of town. Since turning off the main road, she'd only spotted one farmhouse, and it looked deserted.

As they rode over the bumpy gravel road, she strained to hear what Anthony and Abby were saying in the front seat, but she couldn't make out their words. From the tone of Anthony's voice, though, she knew he was still upset with Abby. Every once in a while the sound of a sob drifted back to her, and she realized Abby was crying as she pleaded with Anthony about something. Callie assumed their conversation still centered on whether or not Abby would be permitted to end her association with Anthony and his henchmen. So far, it didn't appear Abby had been successful.

The car slowed and pulled into the driveway of a run-down farmhouse. Callie moved closer to the window and squinted into the darkness to get a better view of her surroundings as they came to a stop.

The house didn't look too different from the other farmhouse they'd passed on the way there. Three steps led up to a front porch where the remains of a waist-high railing with posts lay scattered about. Several panes of glass in the windows were missing, and the roof sagged as if in search of the porch posts that had once supported its weight.

Anthony and Abby climbed from the car, and Callie waited, hardly daring to breathe, to see what they were going to do.

Abby walked around the car to where Anthony stood by the driver's side and stopped next to him. Her raised voice trembled with anger. "You have to be out of your mind bringing me out here. I'm an A.D.A. I can't be directly involved in any of your activities."

His laugh sent cold chills racing up Callie's spine. "Don't kid yourself. You're already involved. You stepped over that line a long time ago when you took the first payment to ensure one of my guys never saw the inside of a jail. It's been downhill for you ever since. You just haven't realized it."

A loud sob tore from Abby's throat. "Please, Anthony. I want to go home."

"Later. First we've got something to do."

He whirled around and jerked the back door of the car open. "Get out, Callie."

She scooted as far away as she could across the seat and cowered next to the window. "No."

He sighed and shook his head. "You can make this hard, or you can choose to make it easy. Get out, or I'll drag you out. And I will be none too gentle about it."

Callie debated what she should do. Common sense told her there was no escape. Finally, she slid back across the seat and stepped out into the farmhouse yard. Anthony wrapped his fingers around her upper arm and squeezed so hard she winced in pain.

Cursing under his breath, he strode to the front porch steps with her in tow. She stumbled up the steps and glanced around wildly for an avenue of escape. Her gaze lit on a large piece of machinery at the end of the porch, and she blinked. A bulldozer? What was it doing here?

Anthony shoved the door open and pulled her into the house. A musty odor assaulted her nostrils. Glancing around the small room they'd entered, a couch and two chairs appeared to be the only furniture in the room. They looked as if they belonged in a landfill.

Anthony didn't stop but propelled her through the room and down a hallway with a door on each side. He stopped at the door on the right, opened it and with a hard shove, pushed her inside. The force sent her reeling across the floor and into a table that sat in the center of the room. She straightened up just as the door closed and a lock clicked.

She ran across the floor and pulled on the doorknob, but it was no use. The door was bolted from the outside. There was no escape that way. Across the room she could make out the shape of a window, and she ran toward it. She grabbed the bottom of the window frame and pulled, but it wouldn't budge.

Callie gazed around the dark room. A ladder-backed chair sat against the wall across the room. She dashed to the chair, picked it up and hurried back to the window. Grasping the back of the chair, she swung it with all her force at the window. The glass shattered and fell to the floor.

She raked the remaining pieces of glass from the window and prepared to climb out when her heart broke into as many pieces as the scattered glass.

Iron bars, bolted to the house, blocked her way.

She stared at the bars for a moment before she turned away and picked up the chair. She sat it upright at the table and dropped down into it. Crossing her arms on the table, she laid her head on them and thought about Seth. Had he missed her yet? If he had, maybe he was already looking for her. Had he found Marty? Was the lieutenant even still alive? If so, he could tell Seth what had happened. But even with that information, how could Seth ever find her at this deserted farm?

Her thoughts turned to her uncle, and she wondered how he was doing tonight. She and Seth had planned to go back by the hospital and see him on their way home when she was finished at the shelter. Now she would never see him again because she was about to die. A tear slipped from her eye, and she wiped at it.

Regret for all the things she should have done during her life flashed into her mind. There were many, but her biggest regret had to do with Seth. She wished she had told him the truth about why she wouldn't marry him. If he'd known she couldn't have children, maybe he could have accepted the chance for a rich life with someone else. But she would never know. If only she had the chance again, she would gladly tell him.

She sat up straight in her chair and stared past the iron bars on the window to the outside of the house. She rose to her feet, walked to the window and looked up into the overcast sky. Her fingers wrapped around the bars, and thoughts of the time she'd spent with Seth lately drifted through her mind.

She'd always known he was a good person, but the past week he had put aside his anger toward her and had done everything he could to make the ordeal with her uncle easier. In her heart she knew what had enabled him to do that—it was the faith he lived by each day. She'd seen it in his mother's life, too. She had welcomed Callie into her home and gone way beyond what one would have expected in trying to help her get through a difficult time.

Seth and Uncle Dan, too, had tried many times to tell her about their faith and about how much God loved her, but she'd refused to listen. She'd blamed God for taking her father and mother and for allowing her to be injured to the point where she could never be a mother. Now, as she faced death in a remote farmhouse, she was completely alone.

Even as the thought entered her head, she remembered Seth once saying that God was always with us. *When we're going through the worst times in our lives, He doesn't abandon us,* Seth had said. *He stays close and gives us peace to endure what must come.* Could He do that for her now? Could He help her face death in a courageous way?

She hadn't prayed since she was a small child and had begged God to save her mother, but now she felt the need for comfort. Seth and his mother appeared to rely on that. Maybe she should try it, too.

She leaned her head against the iron bars and closed her eyes. "God, I haven't talked to You in a long time, but Seth says You're always there if we just reach out. Just be with me and help me face whatever is about to happen. And God, be with Seth. Don't let him blame himself for this. Just help him be happy."

Callie inched closer to the window, and the glass on the floor crunched beneath her feet. The night air drifted into the room, and she inhaled the sweet smell of honeysuckle from nearby. The aroma spread through her body, and in its wake a feeling of peace like she'd never known filled her. Was this what trusting God felt like?

Before she could question herself further, loud voices rang out from the front of the house. She rushed to the door and pressed her ear against it in an attempt to hear what was being said.

"I won't do it!" Abby Dalton's shrill cry pierced the quiet.

"Yes, you will." The angry tone of Anthony's voice chilled her.

"You can't make me! I'm leaving!"

"Oh, no, you're not. I'm not about to let you mess up a good thing. Now sit back down!"

"No!" The sound of running footsteps echoed through the house.

"Come back here, Abby!"

Callie pressed her ear closer to the door, but she jumped away and covered her mouth with her hand at the sharp crack of a gun followed by Abby's scream. The silence that followed sent shivers racing through her body, but it was the sound of heavy footsteps outside the door to her room that paralyzed her with fear.

She backed up against the wall and held her breath as the door swung open. Anthony stood there, staring into the room. "Are you ready, Callie?"

The memory of moments ago, asking God to help her face whatever she must, made her straighten her back and push away from the wall. She clenched her fists at her sides and took a step toward the man she'd always considered a close friend.

"Anthony, if you're going to kill me, I think you owe me the explanation of what this is all about. What are you involved in and why are you doing this?"

He stared at her for a moment before he stepped into the room and closed the door behind him. He kept the gun trained on her as he moved closer. "I'm only protecting myself,

Callie. If you and Dan had just left it all alone, everything would have been all right."

Callie frowned. "Left what alone?"

"Hope's identity. I tried to get him to drop the case years ago, but he wouldn't listen to me. He was determined to find out who she was."

"B-but I don't understand. What does she have to do with all this?"

Anthony sighed and shook his head. "Dan and I were young cops trying to make the next step up the ladder, but it wasn't coming for me fast enough. I needed more money than I was making, and I couldn't wait any longer for a promotion. So I enlisted a few guys I'd arrested once or twice, guys like Carlos Allen, and we began a little extortion scheme. We offered protection to small-business owners in exchange for payment."

"Protection from whom?"

Anthony laughed. "That was the beautiful part. Protection from us. All they had to do was pay us each week, and we wouldn't show up to wreck their stores or rough up their customers. Let that happen a few times, and you're out of business."

Callie glared at him. "So you preyed on small-business owners, people who made little money to start with, and you got rich."

"Something like that. The money began to

add up, and we branched out. One guy who owned a small convenience store right off the interstate decided he didn't want to pay anymore. When Carlos and I showed up one night at his stop-and-shop, he had his nephew, who was a cop, waiting for us. When he stepped out of the back room with his gun aimed at us, I had to defend myself. So I shot and killed him."

Callie's eyes grew wide. "You killed a fellow officer?"

"Yeah, he left me no choice. But that wasn't the trickiest part. A woman traveling through to California had stopped to get some coffee to keep her awake and walked in just as I fired the gun. She tried to run, but Carlos caught her and put her in the back of my police car. We knew we couldn't leave two witnesses, so we killed the store owner and set the place on fire. Then we brought the woman here, killed her and dumped her in the river."

"That was Hope! You killed her, too!"

He shrugged. "I did what I had to do at the time. Carlos drove her car out here, and I used my bulldozer to bury her car by the barn. I thought we'd erased all traces of her, but I was wrong. I never dreamed her body would wash up on shore."

Callie's stomach roiled. This was what she had wanted—to find out the truth behind Hope's murder. But she hadn't suspected the answer had been staring her uncle in the face for years. "And then you pretended to investigate the case of a woman you'd killed."

Anthony chuckled. "That was the funniest thing of all. Dan and I were assigned the case completely by chance. I kept telling him we'd never find out who she was, but he was obsessed with that case. It got worse through the years. In a way, I guess I was obsessed, too. I was afraid if he ever found out who she was, something might come to light that would point the finger of suspicion at me. I always had to stay one step ahead of him."

"I suppose that was easy to do because he trusted you. You were his partner, his best friend." Callie spat the words at him.

"I just tried to keep close to what he was doing, like when he got the idea to put her DNA in the database, I offered to do it for him. Then I destroyed it. And when he stumbled onto the information about Carlos at the shelter, he began checking court records and saw how many defendants were being sent there to do community service. He was asking too many questions, and I knew he had to die. When Carlos failed with that assignment and was about to be taken into custody, I had to take him out, too."

"You?" She could hardly believe what he'd just said. "You killed Carlos?"

"Yeah. I was across the street." He cleared his throat and moved closer. "But enough of this talk. I'm going to go out and get everything ready, and then I'll be back for you."

The tone of his voice told her he was planning something sinister. "What are you going to do?"

"I'm going to dig your grave with that bull-dozer. It's an old one, but I've kept it in good working order. It came in real handy when I buried Hope's car out by the old barn. I won't need a hole that big this time, but I'll make it big enough for two so Abby can join you."

Callie gasped and clamped her hand over her mouth. He'd killed Abby, and he was determined to do the same to her. Wide-eyed, she watched as he turned and left the room. The door closed behind him, then she heard the click of the lock.

Although she knew it was useless, she ran to the door and struggled to pull it open. It wouldn't budge. Callie stepped back and pressed her fingertips to her temples. She had to think. Had to find a way out of this room before Anthony came back.

Outside the house the bulldozer cranked, and its headlights lit a path across the yard. Callie stood at the window and watched the big piece of machinery with Anthony at the controls rumble across the yard. Just before he reached the barn, he stopped, released the blade on the front of the dozer and began to scoop away at the earth.

Callie wanted to move away from the window, but she couldn't. She stood and stared as the hole where she would soon be buried grew larger. Her fingers tightened on the iron bars over the window, and she swallowed the bile that rose in her throat. With each scoop of dirt being dug up, the last minutes of her life were quickly ticking away.

FOURTEEN

Seth stopped the car at the turnoff onto the road that led toward the river levee. He'd hiked this area many times when he was growing up and knew from this point to the levee there weren't many houses.

A sheriff's patrol car waited at the side of the gravel road that wound into the distance. Seth jumped from his car, and the police cruiser that had followed him from Dorothy's house stopped behind him. The sheriff's deputy climbed from his car as Seth approached.

"We were told to meet you guys out here. What kind of problem do we have?"

As quickly as possible Seth told him about the rogue cop who had wounded an officer and was believed to be holding a woman captive at a farm down the road. "This is all connected to an extortion ring that's active in the city and an unsolved twenty-five-year-old murder."

The deputy nodded. "Glad we can help you out. How do you want to handle this?"

Seth debated the options for a moment. "I think we need to move carefully. Since the only way into this area is on this gravel road, he's going to know we've arrived when we drive up. I think we ought to form a barricade with our cars to prevent him from leaving. We'll just have to see what develops after we get there. I'd like him taken alive, though. He has a lot to answer for."

"We'll try," the deputy said. "Since this is our jurisdiction, we'll take the lead. You guys can follow."

Seth nodded and headed back to his car. When the deputy pulled onto the road, Seth followed with the other police cruiser bringing up the rear. As they rounded a curve in the road, a dilapidated farmhouse came into view. He remembered seeing this place when he was a boy and on his way down to the river.

Without warning, lights swept across the yard of the house, and he frowned. Where did they come from? As they drove closer, he saw the cause—a bulldozer scooped away at the earth as it grated up chunks of the yard.

They pulled their vehicles to a stop. The headlights of their cars cut a large swath across the yard. The bulldozer motor idled for a moment as Seth and the officers jumped from their cars and pulled their guns. What was he doing at this time of night, digging a hole in the ground?

At that moment the dozer made a quarter turn and Seth gritted his teeth at the sight of Anthony in the driver's seat. A look of surprise flashed on Anthony's face as he spied the officers who'd fanned out to form a barrier to prevent an escape. He hesitated only a moment before he turned the steering wheel and swung the bulldozer around in a circle. He stopped and sat there facing them as they walked toward him with their guns drawn.

Seth aimed his gun directly at Anthony as one of the sheriff's deputies shouted above the roar of the engine, "Put your hands up and come down. You're under arrest."

Anthony let his gaze drift over the officers facing him, but he said nothing. Then he revved the engine and rumbled forward as fast as the dozer would go. The officers held their ground and kept their guns aimed at him as the machine with the big blade across the front bore down on them.

It was impossible to know which way he was going to steer the big dozer, and Seth didn't know whether to stand still or jump to the side. Then he saw Anthony grimace and lean forward over the steering wheel. With a new burst of speed he drove toward Seth.

"Stop!" Seth yelled, but it did no good. Anthony appeared committed to a course, and there was no stopping him.

"Detective!" one of the deputies shouted. "Get out of the way. He's going to run you over."

With the dozer only inches away, Seth fired at Anthony and took a flying leap away from the dozer. His ankle scraped across the end of the blade, and he landed facedown in the dirt. Ignoring the pain in his leg, Seth jumped to his feet and stared in horror at the scene before him.

The bullet must have found its target, because Anthony lay slumped over the steering wheel of the dozer as it lumbered across the yard, headed toward the side of the house. It looked as if it picked up speed the closer it came to the house. The thought popped into Seth's head that Anthony's foot must be pressed down on the gas pedal when he'd been shot.

The headlights of the machine lit up the side of the house, and Seth thought he saw movement at one of the windows. He narrowed his eyes and tilted his head to one side. What was that? The breath left his body as if he'd been kicked in the stomach. Callie stood at a broken window, her fingers wrapped around iron bars, and stared at the bulldozer bearing down on her.

"Callie!" he screamed. "Get away from there!"

Unmoving, she stood still, the lights illuminating her figure as she remained frozen in disbelief at what was coming toward her.

"Callie!" he screamed again, but his voice was muffled by the sound of the dozer. He had to get to her.

He willed his legs to move, and he sprinted toward the house, but he was no match for the powerful machine. With a thunderous crash, the dozer plowed into the side of the house. The walls collapsed like a house of cards and splintered into thousands of pieces. The dozer disappeared into the house, and there was another crash and then silence.

A cloud of dust rolled from inside, enveloping everything in its path. Seth stopped at the opensided building and stared inside. There was no sign of Callie. The powdery dust from the crash choked him, and he coughed, but he didn't hesitate to move forward as he leaped onto the pile of debris left behind.

"Callie! Where are you?"

The other officers ran up. One of them handed him a flashlight off his utility belt. "Use this. Do you see her anywhere?"

He swept the beam of light in an arc around the room, but all he could see was the scattered remains of the walls and floor of the house. "Callie!" he called again.

He waited, but there was no answer. With his heart pounding in his chest, he crawled through the opening in the house and swept the light around again. The bulldozer had stopped when it crashed into the wall on the other side of the house. Anthony's body was still draped across the steering wheel, but there was no sign of Callie.

The deputies pushed around him and hurried over to the dozer. One of them crawled up and placed his fingers on Anthony's neck. "He's still alive. We'll take care of him. See if you can find his accomplice or the woman he abducted."

Seth stood in the middle of what had once been a room and took a deep breath. "Callie!" he yelled. "Please answer me!"

He waited for a reply, but none came.

She had to be here somewhere, but where? His knees went weak at the horrible possibility of what could have happened. Had she been run over by the dozer and dragged along underneath the big machine? He turned and stared at the bulldozer. What if her body was underneath?

The officers rushed past him and ran toward the wrecked dozer, but all Seth could do was stare helplessly at the piles of rubble. Within minutes the deputies had Anthony stretched out on what remained of the floor. Now was the time to see if Callie was underneath that monstrous machine, but he couldn't move. What would he do if he found her mangled body? He shook his head and took a step backward.

One of the policemen who'd accompanied him to the farm stepped up next to him. "Detective, are you all right?"

Before Seth could respond, a rustling sound to his right caught his attention, and he turned his head to stare. A large pile of debris lay scattered across the floor. He swept the flashlight beam across the splintered pieces of wood, and then he saw movement.

"Callie!" he yelled as he leaped across the floor to what had once been the side wall of the room. Then he heard it again, a muted cry that sounded like a puppy's whimper. "Help me," he yelled to the others as he dropped to his knees.

An officer joined him, and together they dug into the pile of debris. Her arm appeared first, and he paused only long enough to check her pulse and then say a quick thanks to God that she was alive. He tore into the pile again.

Within minutes they had uncovered her entire body and lifted the ceiling beam that had fallen on her and pinned her to the floor. He pressed his trembling fingers to her neck and breathed a sigh of relief when he felt a pulse.

"How is she?" the officer asked.

"She's alive, but she needs medical attention. What about Captain Wilson?"

"He's unconscious. The sheriff's deputies have called for an ambulance. It should be here any minute. There's something else, too. My partner just found the body of A.D.A. Abby Dalton in the other room. She'd been shot."

Seth wrapped his fingers around Callie's and stared into her face. "And she would have been next if we hadn't gotten here in time."

He closed his eyes and offered up a silent prayer. *God, please don't let her die. I have to let her know I forgive her for hurting me and that I still love her. She doesn't have to love me in return, but please let her live.*

Callie tried to open her eyes, but she couldn't. She tried again, but it was no use. Where was she? Something told her she needed to get up, but she couldn't make her body move.

Her eyelids stilled, and she had almost fallen back asleep when she heard a voice. She frowned and tried to concentrate on what it was saying, but it sounded so far away, almost like it was echoing from a distant mountain. But that couldn't be. There were no mountains in Memphis.

The voice called again, this time closer. She strained to hear what it was saying.

"Callie."

Her heart fluttered. The memory of Anthony headed toward her on a bulldozer returned, and she shivered. Seth had come to help her. She had to get to him.

Her voice wouldn't work right, and the words came out in a whisper. She swallowed and tried again. "Seth."

Did he hear her? She waited a moment, and then someone touched her hand. "Callie," Seth said, "lie still. There's an ambulance coming. We'll have you on your way to the hospital in a few minutes."

She opened her eyes and stared up into his face. "You came for me," she whispered.

He smiled and tightened his hold on her hand. "Of course I came for you. I love you, Callie. I want you to know I don't expect anything from you. You don't have to love me in return, but I have to let you know."

Tears filled her eyes, and she put her other hand on top of his. "There are things I have to tell you, Seth, but they can wait until later."

He nodded. "Yes, after you're better."

The memory of Anthony telling her he was going to kill her returned, and she cringed. "What about Anthony?"

Seth glanced across the shattered house. "He's injured, but I think he'll live."

"He killed her," she said.

"I know. We found Abby's body in the other room."

She shook her head. "Not Abby. He killed Hope."

Seth's eyebrows arched, and his mouth dropped open. "Hope?"

"Yes. Her car is buried beside the barn. He used that bulldozer to do it. He was digging a grave for Abby and me."

"B-but why Hope?"

Callie took a deep breath and told him what Anthony had confessed to her before he left to go dig her grave. Seth's expression changed from shock to anger as she talked.

"And all these years he tried to stay one step ahead of Uncle Dan to keep his crimes covered up."

When she finished, Seth exhaled and shook his head. "I can't believe he'd be involved in something like this. Not only was he Dan's friend, he is an officer of the law. He sold out everything that his friends and fellow officers thought he stood for. I don't imagine the justice system is going to go too easy on him."

"Detective Dawtry?"

Callie glanced up into the face of an officer she didn't recognize. "Yes?" Seth said.

"The ambulance just turned off the highway onto the gravel road. ETA is two minutes."

"Thanks." He glanced back down at Callie. "I'll stay with you until you leave with the ambulance. Then I need to help with this crime scene. I'll see you later. You said you had some things to tell me."

She hoped her smile distracted him from the tears in her eyes. "I do."

He tilted his head to one side and leaned closer. "Callie, whatever it is. I know we can work it out."

Before she could respond, one of the deputies touched his shoulder. "The ambulance just turned into the yard."

Seth nodded and rose to his feet. "Call the sheriff and tell him we need some heavy digging equipment out here. There's a car buried beside the barn, and we have reason to believe it's connected to an unsolved murder investigation we've been working on for twenty-five years."

"I'll get right on it."

The deputy turned away and pulled out his cell phone just as two EMTs hurried into the demolished room. They dropped down beside her and began to check her for injuries. As they worked, she tried to catch sight of Seth, but the EMTs blocked her view.

Within minutes she was loaded onto a gurney and rushed toward the front yard where two ambulances sat with their lights flashing. As she was being shoved into the back of one, Seth ran up to the back door.

"Maybe the next time I see you, I'll have all the answers about Hope."

She nodded and smiled at him. "Good. I'll see you then."

One of the EMTs jumped in beside her and slammed the back doors shut. She heard the other one climb in the driver's seat, and before she knew it, they were racing down the road toward the city.

She thought of the last time she'd been in an ambulance. Uncle Dan had been injured, and she'd ridden with him. Although she'd dreaded it that night, she'd known Seth would be at the hospital. He would be there again this time, too—and once again, she dreaded seeing him. He said he loved her, but she hadn't been able to say those words. If she could help it, she still wasn't going to tell him how much she loved him. Not when she'd have to give him up again.

Instead, she planned to tell him why she hadn't married him and then give him his freedom as she had done once before. This time he probably never would forgive her, but it had to be done.

It was time for the truth.

FIFTEEN

Callie opened her eyes and frowned. Where was she? Then she remembered. The hospital. She'd been brought here from the farm last night and had finally been put into this room after being examined in the emergency room, the same place she'd been only a week ago when she and Uncle Dan had been in the wreck.

She turned her head on the pillow toward the window beside her bed. A few beams of sunlight peeked through the closed blinds, and she wondered what time it was. She tried to push up into a sitting position, but every muscle in her body screamed in agony. She exhaled and lay back.

"Good morning, Callie. Do you need me to call the nurse?"

The quiet voice shocked her, and she turned her head toward the other side of the bed. Seth's mother stood beside her, a smile on her face. "Mrs. Dawtry, what are you doing here?"

"Seth called me last night and told me what

had happened. He wanted me to be here with you until he could come. He didn't want you to be alone when you woke up, but evidently, there was a lot for him to clear up about your abduction."

"Yes." Tears filled her eyes. "I thought of Anthony as family. How could he have done this to Uncle Dan and his fellow officers? He was ready to kill me without the least hesitation. I think he did shoot Abby. Do you know if she lived or not?"

"From what Grace reported on TV this morning, Abby was dead at the scene. Anthony is in this hospital, too, but he's under arrest and under guard."

"Good." Another thought popped into her head. "What about Lieutenant Weaver? Anthony shot him when he tried to help me at the shelter."

"He's here in the hospital, too, and lucky to be alive. It's a good thing Seth found him before he bled to death. Marty was able to tell Seth what had happened at the shelter."

"And my uncle? Have you heard anything about his condition this morning?"

She smiled. "His pastor came by to see you earlier, right after he had been up to see Dan. He said the nurses reported his vital signs were much stronger, and he showed some response during the night. Maybe after breakfast one of the nurses can take you in a wheelchair to see him. Maybe he'd respond even more to you."

"Oh, that is good news. And you say his pastor came by to see me?"

"Yes. His name is Pastor Walters. He said he'd come back later today."

"Good. I need to talk to him about an experience I had."

Mrs. Dawtry's eyebrows arched. "A good one or a bad one?"

"It was definitely a good one. For the first time I came to know what you and Seth meant when you talked about the peace that God can give us. That was what got me through the whole ordeal with Anthony."

Mrs. Dawtry put her hand on Callie's arm and squeezed. "I'm glad, Callie. I want you to be happy. I want Seth to be happy, too. He's my son, and I don't want to see him hurt again."

"I know, and neither do I. I think it's time he and I really talk about my reasons for not marrying him. Maybe after that he can let go of the past and move on with his life. I want that for him more than anything."

Seth's mother stared at her as a small frown wrinkled her forehead. "Callie, that sounds almost like you love my son."

"I do, but I'm not going to change my mind

about the two of us. He deserves someone a lot better than me, and I intend for him to have it."

"B-but if you love him, why…"

The door opened, and a nurse walked in. She smiled when she saw that Callie was awake. "Good morning. How are you feeling?"

"Like I was hit by a bus."

The nurse laughed. "From what I hear it was a bulldozer, but don't worry. We'll have you up and around in no time. Now how about some breakfast and then a bath?"

"I'd like that."

Mrs. Dawtry picked up her purse and smiled at Callie. "I'm going down to the cafeteria for some breakfast, too, but I'll be back."

"You don't have to do that," Callie protested. "I'll be fine."

"I promised Seth I'd stay until he got here, and I will. See you in a little while."

Callie watched Seth's mother leave and thought about the conversation they'd just had. Then she thought of how she'd prayed when she was alone in that room at the farm. God had taken care of her then, and she knew He would now.

Telling Seth the truth was going to be hard, but she would do it. She had to give him the chance for the life he deserved. Then as soon as her uncle was able, she would take him with her to Virginia, and she would concentrate on her uncle and her life with him.

Now all she had to do was convince Seth that her plan was the best for both of them.

Seth stopped outside the closed door of Callie's hospital room and rubbed his hands over his eyes. His head ached from the lack of sleep, and his stomach growled. The cup of coffee and granola bar he'd eaten early this morning had done little to satisfy his hunger. But sleep and food were the last things on his mind at the moment. Although his mother had assured him Callie was fine, he couldn't wait to get here and see her.

Taking a deep breath, he pushed the door open and stepped into the room. Callie sat in a chair by the end of her bed. She looked up from the magazine she'd been reading when he entered and smiled. His mother jumped up from her chair and hurried over to him.

She stopped in front of him and stared up into his face. A worried expression flickered in her eyes. "Seth," she said, "you look like you're about to fall asleep on your feet."

He chuckled and raked his hand through his hair. "That's not the first time I've heard you say that to me when I've come in from a crime scene, but I'm okay today."

"I'm glad. We've been worried about you."

His gaze traveled over to Callie. "It took me a while to get some of the loose ends tied up, but I'm here now."

His mother turned and picked up her purse. "So you are, and I think that's my signal to get out of here and leave the two of you alone." She walked over to Callie and kissed her on the cheek. "I'm glad you're doing so well. I'll be back. But I want you to know that when you're released, I expect you to come back to our house."

Callie smiled up at his mother. "Thank you, Mrs. Dawtry. We'll see."

His mother nodded and then patted him on the arm as she walked past him to the door. When she'd left, he took the chair she'd been sitting in and pulled it over next to Callie. He sat down and took her hand in his.

"I could hardly keep my mind on what I was doing this morning because I kept thinking about you and how close Anthony came to carrying through on his plan. I don't know what I would have done if…"

He choked up, and Callie tightened her grip on his hand. "Don't think about that. You were able to save me. How did you find me?"

She listened as he told her about hearing the gunshot, rushing to the shelter and how everything had happened from there. "Throughout the whole ordeal, I don't think I ever quit praying that I'd find you alive. Since then, I've thanked God over and over for taking care of you."

She smiled. "I was praying, too, Seth. I found that comfort and peace in turning my troubles over to God that you and your mother have. I didn't know whether I'd live or die, but I knew that God was with me until the end. And I prayed for you, too."

Her words surprised him. "You did? Did you pray that I'd find you?"

"I suppose I did. But my main prayer for you was that you would have a good life. That's what I've always wanted for you."

A warning triggered in his mind and radiated through his body. She'd said she had things to tell him, and it seemed she was about to do it. The tone of her voice, though, made him realize he might not like what he was about to hear. He tried to pull his hand away, but she held if fast.

"Is that why you wouldn't marry me? So I could have a good life?"

"Yes."

He'd expected her to deny it, and her answer stunned him. "That makes no sense. The reason you didn't marry me is because you didn't want to be married to a policeman."

She sighed and bit down on her lip for a moment. "I knew you thought that, and I let you believe it. But there was another reason."

"Then tell me what it was."

She took a deep breath. "I thought someone else could give you the life you deserved. I couldn't do that."

"Why?"

"Because…"

"Answer me, Callie." She flinched from his stern tone.

"Because I…I…"

His head pounded, and he groaned. This had dissolved into a repeat of what had happened between them two years ago. He had pressed her for an answer, and she had refused to give him one. He'd promised himself he'd be patient with her, but he was exhausted and strained to his last nerve. Unable to stop himself, he pushed to his feet and glared down at her.

"I told you last night at the farm how I feel about you, and I had hoped that you might feel the same way. I'm not going to go through this again. Tell me now what is so hard for you to say or I'm out of here for good."

Tears gushed from her eyes. Her lips moved, but no words came out.

Seth whirled and strode across the room, needing to leave before he said something he'd really regret. He'd just grabbed the doorknob when her agonized cry stopped him in his tracks.

"I can't have children!" she sobbed.

For a moment he couldn't move, then he thought he must not have heard her right. He turned, walked back and dropped into the chair. "What did you say?"

Her shoulders shook. "Two weeks before you asked me to marry you, I went to the doctor and found out I can never have children."

"B-but why?"

Fresh tears slid down her face. "I told you about the car hitting me on my bicycle when I was a child. I had severe pelvic injuries, and the scar tissue that developed makes it impossible for me to get pregnant."

A box of tissues sat on the table beside her. He reached for one and wiped at the tears on her face. "Why didn't you tell me?"

She looked up, a stricken expression on her face. "Because I knew you'd insist it didn't make a difference, but it did—it *does*. You deserve to be a father, and I couldn't steal that from you."

He leaned back in his chair and shook his head. "So you decided to make a decision for me that should have been mine to make."

"No, I wanted to help you. I wanted you to find a woman who could give you children. It's what would make you truly happy—happier than I could ever make you. I saw you at the hospital the other day with that boy you coach, and I saw how you acted with Brad and Laura's son. If we had married, you would have come to hate me because I can't give you what you deserve."

She shoved her clenched fists into her lap and stared down at them. "Callie," he said. "Look at me." He waited, but she didn't look up. He spoke louder. "Callie, I said look at me."

She glanced up. "What?"

"Do you love me?" She started to speak but hesitated. "Tell me the truth. Do you love me?"

She exhaled a big breath. "Yes. I thought I'd gotten over you until I came home, but I hadn't."

He leaned forward and covered her fists with his hands. "I love you, too, and I want you in my life. I want more than that. I want you as my wife."

She shook her head. "You don't understand..."

He placed his finger on her lips. "No, you're the one who has it all wrong. You think I can't be a father unless it's a child of my own? Have you forgotten how Dan has been the father I always wanted? Don't you think I could do that, too?"

She frowned. "How?"

He chuckled and shook his head. "I always thought you were the smartest woman I'd ever known, but I'm not so sure anymore. There are a lot of options available to couples who can't have children. Adoption, foster parenting, in vitro fertilization and who knows what else. Those are things to be explored in the future. First off, we have to decide how we feel."

"What do you mean?"

He took a deep breath. "Well, you wanted me to be happy so badly that you walked out on me, and I lived through the two unhappiest years of my life. From what I guess, yours haven't been that great, either. Am I right?"

"Yes."

"Then we have to do something about that. I think I heard you say you love me. Do you?"

She nodded. "I do, Seth, but I want you to be happy."

"Then marry me and take away all the unhappiness I've had for the past two years. I love you, and I promise you, we'll face this problem together. How about it?"

Her lips trembled, and more tears filled her eyes. "Are you sure?"

"More than I've ever been about anything in my life. Please marry me, Callie."

"Nothing would make me happier."

His heart soared as he pulled her to him and pressed his lips against hers. She put her arms around his neck and pulled him closer as if to seal the commitment they'd just made to each other.

A discreet cough behind them brought him back to the present, and he pulled away to look over his shoulder. A smiling nurse stood just inside the door. "It seems you're feeling better than the last time I checked."

Callie laughed. "It's the best I've felt in years."

"That's good to hear," she said. "I came to tell you that your uncle has regained consciousness and is asking for you. Would you like to go see him?"

She clasped Seth's hand and smiled. "Oh, Seth, this is the best day of my life."

He squeezed her hand. "Mine, too."

"I'll get a wheelchair and be right back," the nurse said as she scooted out the door.

Callie reached up and trailed the tip of her finger down his cheek. "I never dreamed we could get back together. Are you sure you want to do this?"

"With all my heart." He was about to say more, but his cell phone rang. He pulled it from his pocket and pressed it to his ear. "Hello."

"Seth, this is Brad. I wanted to call you with some news."

He pushed to his feet and frowned. "Bad or good?"

"Good news. They were able to uncover

Hope's car and pull it out of the hole where Anthony had buried it. There was a suitcase in the trunk, and it had all her identification in it."

"That *is* good news. What is her name?"

"Her name is Valerie Traywick, and she's from a little town in West Virginia. There were several pictures in the bag of her with a small boy who we think must be her son. We're hoping the lab can come up with some more DNA from her clothes so it can be entered in the national database. In the meantime, we've got people in touch with the West Virginia authorities trying to locate any family she might have."

Seth closed his eyes and let out a long breath. "Dan has searched all these years, and the answers were so close. Keep me posted."

"Okay."

Seth disconnected the call and smiled at Callie. "Her name is Valerie Traywick, and she's from West Virginia."

Before Callie could answer him, the nurse entered, pushing a wheelchair. "Here we are. Ready to go see your uncle?"

Callie held out her hand, and Seth helped her to her feet. "Thank you for not giving up on Valerie or on me. Uncle Dan is going to be so happy."

He leaned over and kissed her on the cheek. "Let's go tell him together."

SIXTEEN

Two weeks later Callie spooned the last bite of applesauce into her uncle's mouth and smiled. "I think your appetite is improving every day. Keep this up, and you'll be out of here in no time."

He scowled at her and shook his head. "The next stop after this is the rehab center. It's going to be weeks before I get to go home."

Callie laughed. "At least you have a place to stay for a while until we decide where we're going to live."

His eyebrows shot up. "What do you mean *we?* You're going to live with Seth after you're married, and I'm going to get a small apartment. I don't need to be taking care of a big house anymore."

She sighed and put the empty applesauce bowl back on the hospital tray. "We have lots of time to decide all that. Seth wants us to rebuild the house where the other one burned, and the three of us live together. I think that's a good idea."

He shook his head. "We can rebuild the house, but you and Seth will live there alone. I'm going to an apartment."

She leaned over and kissed him on the cheek. "You can sure be stubborn when you try."

He laughed. "Who's trying? I'm naturally this way all the time."

She was about to reply when someone knocked on the door and then pushed it open. Seth stuck his head into the room. "Are you up to some company?"

Her uncle motioned for him to come in. "You're not company. You're family."

Seth glanced over his shoulder and then pushed the door open wider. A young man who looked to be in his early thirties stood in the hallway behind Seth. He smiled as Seth ushered him inside. They stopped at the foot of her uncle's bed.

"Dan, Callie, this is Michael Traywick. He's Valerie's son, and he's come to Memphis to take his mother's body home for burial."

Callie sucked in her breath and pushed her fist against her trembling lips as she stared down at her uncle. Tears slipped out of the corners of his eyes, and he held out his hand to Michael. "Come here, son."

Michael walked around the end of the bed and clasped Uncle Dan's hand in his. "I'm so happy to meet you. I can't believe that you have tried for twenty-five years to find out who my mother was and where she came from. How can I ever thank you for answering the questions that have haunted me since I was six years old?"

"Seeing you here and knowing your mother is finally going home is all the thanks I need. But I want to know what she was doing here. Callie has told me what happened after she arrived in Memphis, but we don't know anything else."

Michael pulled up a chair and sat down next to the bed. Callie drifted over to where Seth stood, and he put his arm around her. All three of them listened as Michael began his story.

"I was five years old when my parents divorced. From what my dad's told me, she'd always wanted to get out of West Virginia. When I was six, she convinced him to let me stay with him until she could go to California and get a job. Then she would send for me. She left home and was never heard from again."

"That must have been hard for a little boy," Uncle Dan said.

"Yes, it was. I cried many nights when I was growing up, wondering why my mother didn't love me enough to send for me like she'd said she would. My father told me she didn't care about me, or she would have written. After a while I believed him and began to hate her. Then when I got married and had a son, I began to think about my mother, and I wanted to find her. I entered my DNA in the national database three years ago, but I'd never heard anything until last week when I received word there had been a hit. I finally found out the truth, thanks to you."

Uncle Dan looked up at her and Seth. "And to those two also. They found the missing pieces and pulled everything together. I just kept the interest going all these years."

Michael reached over and squeezed her uncle's hand. "You buried her and placed a tombstone on her grave. I'm forever in your debt."

"No, you're not. Take your mother's body home and bury her where she grew up. And tell your son about a woman named Hope who came to be an important part of a man's life in Tennessee."

"I will. There were several letters in her suitcase she had written to me. She wrote how much she loved me, and that she could hardly wait to get settled in California so I could join her. She said the first thing she'd do would be take me to the beach. There were also several envelopes with pictures of the two of us together. I'll keep those always." He glanced up at Seth. "Detective Dawtry tells me there's a locket in the evidence bin. It has a picture in it of her and me. Maybe someday I'll have a daughter to give it to."

"We'll get that back to you as soon as the trial is over," Seth said.

Michael pushed to his feet. "I hope you'll let me know when that is. I want to come back and face the man in court who robbed me of the most important person in my life when I was a child."

"We will."

Michael shook Uncle Dan's hand once more and walked to the door. "I'll never forget any of you."

"Neither will we forget you," her uncle said.

Michael walked out and closed the door behind him. The three of them were silent for a moment until Dan spoke. "I always knew there had to be someone she loved somewhere. I'm glad he finally has closure."

Seth smiled. "What are you going to do now that you no longer have Hope's case to keep you occupied?"

"I don't know," he said. "I'll have to look for something. It seems the other problem in my life is taken care of."

Callie frowned. "What other problem did you have?"

Uncle Dan grinned. "Getting you two back together. I've been trying to do it for two years.

I'm glad you finally listened to me. The sooner we can get you two married, the happier I'll be."

Callie wrapped her arms around Seth's neck and smiled up at him. "I think we've just been sentenced to life without parole."

Seth laughed, slipped his arm around Callie's waist, and pulled her closer. "And no appeals. I love you, Callie."

"I love you, too, Seth."

She pulled his head down, and his lips pressed against hers. In his kiss she felt the promise of great things yet to come, and she could hardly wait to meet each one with Seth by her side.

* * * * *

Dear Reader,

Every year tens of thousands of people go missing in the United States. Many of them are never found and leave families with unanswered questions about the fates of their loved ones. *Trail of Secrets,* although a fictional story, is loosely based on the real life disappearance of twenty-two-year-old Gloria Faye Stringer in Texas in 1975. Having known her family for many years, I know the heartache they suffered. Through the efforts of one man in Texas who never gave up trying to find out the identity of the young woman whose death he'd investigated as a young police officer, they were finally able to bring their precious Gloria's remains back to Tennessee in 2012 for burial. My prayer is that God will bless the families with missing loved ones and will watch over the valiant law-enforcement officers who seek to find them answers.

Sandra Robbins

Questions for Discussion

1. Dan Lattimer hoped to bring closure to a family by finding out the identity of the young woman whose murder he'd investigated. Have you ever known a family who had a missing loved one? How did you minister to them?

2. What do you as a parent do to teach your children about the dangers of abduction and how to respond to people they don't know?

3. Callie was surprised when she learned about her uncle's case from twenty-five years earlier. How do you feel about family members keeping secrets from each other?

4. Callie showed great courage when she attacked the man who was trying to smother her uncle. How do you think you'd react if you saw someone trying to hurt or kill a member of your family?

5. Seth's father abandoned their family when Seth was young. Have you had to deal with an absent parent in your life? How did you cope?

6. Callie wouldn't marry Seth because she couldn't have children. Have you or anyone you've known had to deal with infertility? How did it affect you?

7. Anthony pretended for years to be Dan's best friend. Have you ever been deceived by someone you trusted? What did you do when you uncovered the truth?

8. Although Peggy worked at the homeless shelter, she showed little concern for the emotional well-being of the people who came there. Have you ever volunteered in a homeless shelter? What can Christians do to help the homeless in the cities and towns where we live?

9. As an Assistant District Attorney, Abby violated the trust put in her by participating in illegal activities. Have you ever known a public official who took advantage of his/her position? What happened to them?

10. Michael Traywick missed out on twenty-five years of making memories with his mother when she disappeared. Are you taking advantage of the time you have with your loved ones? What are some ways you are helping your family to have happy lives?

LARGER-PRINT BOOKS!

GET 2 FREE LARGER-PRINT NOVELS
PLUS 2 FREE MYSTERY GIFTS

Love Inspired

Larger-print novels are now available...

LARGER-PRINT BOOKS!

GET 2 FREE
LARGER-PRINT NOVELS
PLUS 2 FREE
MYSTERY GIFTS

Love Inspired®
SUSPENSE
RIVETING INSPIRATIONAL ROMANCE

Larger-print novels are now available...